WHITAKER BANK

A Subsidiary of Whitaker Bank Corporation

Dear Fellow Kentuckian,

At Whitaker Bank Corporation, we're extremely proud to provide state-of-the-art banking services with a personal, friendly touch throughout the Commonwealth.

We're also very proud to sponsor this book about Cawood Ledford's career. Cawood has contributed greatly to our state. This book is a testament to his accomplishments, both as a legendary sports announcer and as a person.

Sincerely,

Elmer Whitaker

Elmer Whitaker
President

P.O. Box 13010 • 2311 Paris Pike • Lexington, Kentucky 40505 • (606) 299-9200

Heart of Blue

by Cawood Ledford

Host Communications, Inc.
Lexington, Kentucky

"Heart of Blue" is published and printed by Host Communications, Inc., 904 North Broadway, Lexington, Kentucky 40505. W. James Host, Publisher; Richard A. Ford, President; Eric Barnhart, Vice President

Photography by Brian Spurlock, David Coyle, Bill Straus, Michael C. Hebert, *Louisville Courier-Journal.* Additional photos provided by the University of Kentucky Media Relations Office.
Project manager: Kim Ramsay
Distribution: Laura Mize
Edited by Pat Henderson and David Kaplan
Cover design and layout by James O. Barker
Editorial assistance by Dave Mrvos, Mike Nayman, Jai Giffin, Craig Baroncelli, Dan Peters, Jim Kelsey, Mark Buerger, Jared Svoboda, Will Roleson, Mark Coyle, Brian Roberts, Pete Rhoda, Lori Holladay
Design assistance by Paulette Ball, Laura Doolittle, Dana Bart, Tammi Geierman, Minna Youart, Tara Yurkshat

ISBN: 1-57640-001-8

Heart of Blue

by Cawood Ledford

To four great Kentucky basketball coaches and also great friends, Adolph Rupp, Joe B. Hall, Eddie Sutton and Rick Pitino.

Introduction

"What is important about a game is not the score but the people who play it."

— *Red Smith*

For 39 years I had the distinct privilege of being courtside when the Kentucky Wildcats took the basketball court for combat. I saw team after team, player after player and four different coaches fashion the Kentucky program into one of the best in all of college basketball.

My first season as the broadcaster, in 1954, was the only undefeated Kentucky team of the modern era. Who could forget the 1958 team, the Fiddlin' Five, who came out of obscurity to win the NCAA title. Two decades later a great UK team, which was to send four starters to the pros, captured the big prize in 1978.

There were other teams who failed to win the game's biggest trophy but were so long on courage and determination that they captured our imagination. The 1992 team, the Unforgettables, comes immediately to mind.

Along the way, there were some great games ... games where it seemed impossible to win but somehow the Cats pulled them out.

Even though my broadcasting career ended with the 1992 season, my interest and affection for UK basketball did not. In recalling my favorite Wildcat memories, how could I fail to chronicle that mind-blowing 31-point comeback to beat LSU or the incredible overtime win over Arkansas in the 1995 SEC Tournament!

I hope you'll enjoy this trip back through the years as we remember some great Kentucky basketball memories.

The Coaches

If any school has had four better basketball coaches over the last half-century than the University of Kentucky, history failed to record it. Adolph Rupp, Joe B. Hall, Eddie Sutton and Rick Pitino have guided the Wildcat fortunes with tremendous success. In my 39 years as the UK broadcaster, I had the privilege of working closely with these distinguished coaches.

I spent 19 years at the microphone while Coach Rupp was running the show from the UK bench. While I worked more years with Rupp than any of the other three, I probably knew him less intimately. Never in all our years together did I call him anything but "Coach Rupp." He was 52 years old when I began broadcasting the Wildcat games and he was already at the very top of the coaching profession. He had already won three NCAA Championships (more than any other coach at the time) and in 1948, he had taken the Fabulous Five to the Olympic Games and won the gold medal.

There is a picture of Coach Rupp in my office at home inscribed, "To my best friend, with kindest regards for many years of working together, Adolph F. Rupp." While I was very flattered and proud of the inscription, never did I think I was his best friend.

Rupp was a very private person. I don't think he had very many

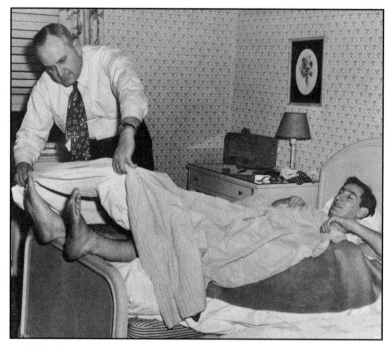

Adolph Rupp's bedside manner included trying to tuck very tall Alex Groza into a very small bed.

close friends, but he had many people he liked and enjoyed being around and I like to think I fit in that group. He was really a family man. He just thought the world of his wife, Esther, and his son, Herky, and when the grandchildren came along, he adored them.

Coach Rupp was the most punctual and the most frugal of the four Kentucky coaches during my time near the program. His long-time assistant, Harry Lancaster, met with every incoming freshman class, with the admonition to not only be on time but be early. He said if the coach said to be somewhere at 2 o'clock, be there at 1:45. You had to keep your watch synchronized if you were operating on Rupp's schedule. When he got on a bus, without even looking around, he uttered his order to move with the words, "kick 'er doc." More than once he left someone in the traveling party, often a player. He ran his schedule with a military precision.

Coach Rupp wasn't exactly a tightwad but he wasn't a spend-thrift, either. He was close with a buck. I always thought it was because he grew up in Kansas during hard times. His father died while Rupp was a young boy and the entire family had to work hard and watch its money carefully. He grew up with a strong work ethic and a strong sense of saving his money.

Of the four Kentucky coaches, Rupp was the best speaker hands down. His speeches were very structured and he was a spellbinder from the podium. He was the best and most entertaining sports figure, as a public speaker, I ever heard, and one of the best from any profession.

Coach Rupp had the greatest influence on me of the four coaches. I was still in my 20s when I first met him and he was at the very pinnacle of his coaching success. He was my mentor and a person I admired very much. I learned a great deal from him. He taught me how to set goals and from him I learned the tremendous importance he attached to being well prepared. I just owe a lot to Coach Rupp.

If ever a man walked into a tougher coaching situation than Joe B. Hall, I don't know his name. Rupp had been at UK for 42 years and had won more games than any coach in history. He was forced out as coach because he was 70 years old. He went kicking and screaming. During his last season, he saw Hall as his only obstacle to keeping his job and that year must have been pure hell for Joe.

To say that my 19-year association with Coach Rupp was the longest of any UK coach is not entirely accurate. Joe B. was on the coaching staff for 20 years while I was the broadcaster but for his first seven years, he served as an assistant coach and was gone much of the time for recruiting and scouting trips. I got to know him very well during those seven years, but I didn't see him as often as I did Coach Rupp.

Hall had been a head coach at Regis College, in Denver, and at Central Missouri State College when he agreed to join Rupp on the UK staff in 1965. He had an immediate impact on the program. Before he went into coaching, Joe had been a salesman and it took one of his best efforts at salesmanship to convince Rupp to install a preseason conditioning program. There were probably other reasons for the improvement, but the team that had gone 15-10 the previous year, had a remarkable turnaround with a 27-2

Melvin Turpin was a big reason Joe B. Hall's 1984 Kentucky team advanced to the Final Four in Seattle.

season and was runner-up for the NCAA Championship. That team will always be known as "Rupp's Runts."

When Joe arrived at Kentucky he also discovered that recruiting was a sort of "fly-by-the-seat-of-the-pants" operation. He carefully organized a recruiting plan and in his first season, Joe brought in a recruiting class of Dan Issel, Mike Pratt, Mike Casey, Jim Dinwiddie and Terry Mills. For the remainder of his tenure at Kentucky, Joe constantly recruited excellent talent. He also really is the man who broke the color line for UK basketball. He did recruit Tom Payne in 1969 while Rupp was still the coach, but Payne went to the pros after one season as a Wildcat. Joe B. is the man who brought in many fine African-Americans under his watch as the head coach.

I got to know Hall while he was an assistant, but when he moved into the top job replacing Rupp in 1972, I thought he really felt the enormous pressure of the job. A few years later after the legendary John Wooden resigned, Joe said UCLA should hire him since he was the only man in coaching experienced at following a legend. He was.

Coach Hall is just now receiving the credit he deserves for his 13 years as the man at the helm of the Wildcats. It was under Hall that Kentucky won the 1978 NCAA Championship. He took the Cats to two other Final Fours. He won the NIT when it was still a first-rate postseason tournament. In 13 years, Joe brought back eight Southeastern Conference Championships to add to UK's over-stuffed trophy case. He truly had a remarkable run as the Kentucky coach.

I first met Eddie Sutton at the 1978 Final Four in St. Louis. It was well-documented that Sutton had taken an Arkansas basketball program that was close to non-existent and built it into one of the strongest in the game. When our paths first crossed, Eddie had brought a fine team to St. Louis to meet Kentucky in the semifinals. The Cats won a hard-fought 64-59 decision on their way to the championship.

I didn't see Sutton again until 1985, in Salt Lake City, and I was surprised he remembered me. Arkansas and Kentucky were among the four teams assembled for the first and second rounds of the NCAA Tournament. I went out with UK for practice the day before the Cats were to meet Washington. Arkansas was just finishing its session as Kentucky was preparing to take the floor. Sutton called out to me and we had a short, pleasant meeting. His team lost the next night while Kentucky won. The Cats beat UNLV to advance to the regional. I was to meet Eddie Sutton again very soon, under very different circumstances.

Kentucky moved on to Denver but lost the first game against St. John's. After the game, Joe B. Hall announced his retirement as the Wildcat coach.

The Final Four was held in Lexington that year and the nation's basketball coaches always conveniently held their convention around the big show. It was during this carnival that UK Athletics Director Cliff Hagan announced Sutton would be the new coach of the Wildcats.

I got to know Eddie well over the next four years. He proved to be an outstanding coach and he was very pleasant to work with. He was the first of the coaches I worked with who had a walk-through on the day of the game. Both Rupp and Hall had shoot-arounds where the team would take shooting practice from the field and from the free throw line. Sutton walked the team through the game plan and had them run their out-of-bounds plays. He also had them defense the out-of-bounds plays he expected the opponent to run. I confess I really enjoyed watching these drills and the very relaxed attitude on game days. After the team completed its walk-through, on the road, he would have some kind of a fun game among the assistant coaches, the media and the traveling party. We had contests from three-point range and we played games of "horse," but as the season wore on, our lack of talent reduced our competition to free throw shooting.

Both Rupp and Hall were very guarded when discussing an op-

Eddie Sutton helped Kentucky capture two SEC Tournament and two league regular season titles in his four years.

ponent on their pre-game radio program, but Sutton was more to the point in his appraisal. He would say that while anything could happen in a game, Kentucky would win eight times out of 10 against a certain team. That was a new approach for a UK coach.

Joe B. certainly didn't leave the cupboard bare and Eddie took good talent and did a masterful job with it. His first season at Kentucky, Sutton took the Wildcats to a 32-4 record that included both the SEC championship and the SEC Tournament championship. The Wildcats went to Charlotte for the NCAA and posted easy wins over Davidson and Western Kentucky to advance to the Southeast Regional at Atlanta.

The Southeast Regional resembled the SEC Tournament. Kentucky, Alabama and LSU were all in the field and, to win the championship and a trip to the Final Four, Kentucky would have to beat both Alabama and LSU for the fourth time that season. The Wildcats defeated the Crimson Tide but fell two points short against LSU, 59-57. It was still a marvelous season and, for his efforts in guiding the team, Sutton was named national Coach of the Year. I think you'll agree ... that was quite a beginning for Eddie as the Wildcats' coach.

Sutton's second year was a rebuilding season as the Wildcats finished with an 18-11 record. The next year, Kentucky rebounded with a super season and had a 23-4 record going into the NCAA Tournament that included both the conference regular season and tournament titles. Once there, the Cats won twice before a poor performance found them losing to Villanova, 80-74. Later, the NCAA was to wipe out UK's NCAA Tournament record and the Southeastern Conference was to strip Kentucky of both conference titles.

Only a few weeks after the season, in April, an Emery Air Freight envelope spilled open on a conveyor belt. Inside was $1,000. The envelope was addressed from Dwane Casey, one of Sutton's assistants, to Claud Mills, father of top recruit Chris Mills.

The NCAA investigated Kentucky throughout the next season,

Pitino's up-tempo style of play helped win the hearts of Cat fans, and also has helped Kentucky win a lot of games.

and it was a nightmare for everyone who cared about the UK program. Kentucky finished the year with a 13-19 record, the first losing season since 1927. Sutton was forced to resign. The happiest moment of the season was when it was finally over.

The first time I ever saw Rick Pitino was at the 1987 Final Four in New Orleans. I didn't get the chance to meet him but I was very impressed with how confident and polished he was for a person so young, as I sat in the audience at the media conferences. I was also impressed with his Providence team. I hadn't seen the Friars play but I knew they shot a lot of threes and I knew they had won a very difficult regional to get to the Final Four.

I had been assigned to work a different regional, but I was well aware of Rick's success in Louisville where his team manhandled an outstanding Alabama team — maybe one of Wimp Sanderson's best — and beat a strong Georgetown team. When I saw Providence lose to Syracuse in the Final Four, I realized just what a great coaching job he had done because the Friars simply did not have the great talent you normally see at a Final Four.

Rick had moved on to the professional ranks with the New York Knicks after the NCAA Tournament and I didn't see him again for two years. He was in Lexington to look over C.M. Newton's offer to be the next UK coach. This time I did meet him. I introduced myself and I'll admit I was pleased that he knew who I was. He told me he had listened to my broadcasts many times while driving through New England on recruiting trips.

I was very pleased when Pitino accepted the coaching job at

Joe B. Hall pointed the way for some very successful Kentucky teams, both as an assistant under Rupp and as the Wildcats' head coach.

Kentucky. The Wildcat program was at the lowest level almost anyone could remember. After the NCAA sanctions, the best players transferred. There would be no TV for a year and no postseason tournaments for two years. Only two starters were among the eight scholarship players that would make up Pitino's first Kentucky team. No player was taller than 6-7. C.M. Newton correctly said it was the poorest UK talent in half a century. I knew Pitino had taken down-and-out programs at other places and built those teams into winners. He would face his biggest challenge to rebuild the Wildcats.

My last three years as the UK broadcaster, Pitino was the coach. I got to know him quite well over that time and I must admit, they were the most enjoyable three years of my 39 with the Wildcats. To see him take a down-and-out program and immediately guide it to over-achieving was just great fun to be associated with. I still think his accomplishments border on a miracle.

I knew that the 1989-90 season, Rick's first at UK, was going to be a bummer. Even though an optimist, he felt he had only two players that were capable of playing at Kentucky's level, Reggie Hanson and Derrick Miller. The other six scholarship players he thought were back-up players at best. Ironically, four of those six became the nucleus of the team that brought Kentucky back to basketball prominence. They were called the "Unforgettables."

When C.M. hired Pitino he gave him a seven-year contract. Newton thought the UK program was in such desperate straits that it would be unreasonable to expect the new coach to rebuild the team on a standard five-year contract. Rick has worked wonders many times in his career, but none was a bigger surprise than when he took his first UK team to a 14-14 record. Not even the biggest optimist, and that probably includes "Mr. Optimism" himself, Rick Pitino, believed he could accomplish so much so soon.

How did he do it? It wasn't just the X's and O's. His coaching philosophy was revealed in his first season and it is a plan he follows today.

To start with, he is the hardest working person I have ever been around. He comes to Memorial Coliseum in the wee hours of the morning and stays until nine or 10 o'clock at night. Rick has a strong work ethic and he expects the same from his players. His teams are always in tremendous physical condition. Kentucky often wins in the last 10 minutes of a game simply because the players are in better physical condition than the opponents. Pitino really gets to know his players — learns what makes them tick. His first season at UK he brought in Frank Gardner, a psychologist who had worked with the Knicks, to test his team. He learned

Rupp was a master of game preparation, which helped him become the all-time winningest coach in Division I men's basketball history.

which players needed prodding and which needed praise. He understood his players and how to deal with them as individuals.

Fans really don't get to know the coaches and there is a side to them the public seldom sees. In Pitino's case I think it is his generosity. He has given generously of his time and money to help his church, his charities and his friends. He is one of the most giving people I have ever known.

Rick was a joy to work with. He had a natural flair for huge crowds. He is a very entertaining person, whether it's one-on-one or before a large crowd.

The four coaches I worked with at the University of Kentucky had different personalities but they shared a lot of philosophies when it came to basketball. Every single one of them was a driven person — driven to win. They all had the fire in their belly when it came to competition.

All four put great emphasis on defense. They employed different styles, but all of them really believed for a team to win it had to start with good solid defense and each of them spent a lot of time in practice stressing the defensive part of the game.

All four put great importance on scouting an opponent. John Wooden, who had such great success at UCLA, was fond of saying he worried about his own team and didn't much care what an opponent did. Coach Rupp surely had to be one of the pioneers of scouting an adversary, and the three men who followed him at UK all put great importance on finding out anything and everything they could about every team on their schedules. I think that with the introduction of videotape most coaches today really stress scouting their basketball enemies.

Rupp and Pitino favored the running game more than did Hall or Sutton. Joe B. did run more often than Sutton's teams but Rupp and Pitino liked to see their teams race up and down the court. Sutton's offense was the most deliberate, requiring several passes before a player put up a shot.

The three-point shot came into being after Rupp and Hall had departed but both Sutton and Pitino embraced the new rule with open arms. Pitino's first UK team set a batch of national records with the three-pointer but as his talent improved, Rick's teams did not fire from behind the arc with as much frequency as his early Kentucky teams did.

Hall and Pitino were the most active recruiters of the four UK coaches. Both of them logged a lot of miles seeking out talent and going into the homes of the recruits. Rupp and Sutton preferred to leave much of the recruiting to their assistants.

Rupp was the most accessible of the UK coaches. Despite all his fame he never had an unlisted telephone number. On a slow news day, you could always get the Baron on the phone for an interview.

Rupp and Pitino were the most charismatic. Each could enter a room and immediately become the center of attention. They were also the most fun and most interesting to interview. Both were very quotable and each had a marvelous sense of humor.

I think I was close to all four Kentucky coaches. I liked and respected each of them and I believe they respected me. I feel very fortunate to have spent most of my adult life around men who were winners and I like to think maybe a little rubbed off on me.

My strangest association was my last. I spent only three years as the broadcaster after Rick Pitino came to the Bluegrass, but I think we developed a very special relationship. I really can't explain it. I'm old enough to be his father, but I think it was more of a friendship that we had than a father-son relationship. I think each of us had a lot of respect for the other. I know I have tremendous respect for Rick both as a coach and a person.

We don't see each other nearly as often as we did while I was the broadcaster, but when we do get together it's amazing to me we seem to pick up right where we left off.

I enjoyed my association with all four of the UK coaches. Coach Rupp was my mentor, Joe B. was my friend, Eddie brought in new wrinkles to the program, Pitino is always a breath of fresh air and, until the NCAA imposed the 20-hour rule, worked the players

Sutton was one coach who was always willing to sit down and visit.

Pitino receives a hug from Mark Pope following the Cats' thrilling comeback win over Arkansas in the 1995 SEC Tournament final.

longer than the others. Coach Rupp had the shortest practices. Sutton brought the walk-through on game day and Pitino took that and put it in fast forward, and sometimes, I thought the walk-through was actually a full practice on game day.

The four Kentucky coaches: Rupp, Hall, Sutton and Pitino were four very different personalities. But they all had one thing in common ... they were driven to win and each of them could flat coach basketball.

The Perfect Season

December 5, 1953, was a red-letter day for the University of Kentucky basketball team and for me. It marked the first time the Wildcats had faced an opponent in 20 months. It was also the very first time that I sat at courtside to report the play-by-play action of the Cats.

Kentucky had been suspended from playing the 1952-53 schedule. UK was one of seven schools implicated in the point-shaving scandal of the late 1940s and, in a bitterly worded indictment handed down by Judge Saul S. Streit, he not only ruled that Kentucky players had taken money to control the point spreads on games, but that Coach Adolph Rupp was a party to subsidizing players illegally.

Rupp was to be proved innocent of charges that he had been involved in gambling and of any manipulation to affect the outcome of a game. University President Herman L. Donovan stood firmly in favor of Rupp at a time when some were calling for Rupp to retire.

The point-shaving scandal had run its course by late summer of 1952, but that October the Southeastern Conference came down hard on the Wildcats, ruling that Kentucky would not be permitted to compete during the 1952-53 season.

Kentucky was not able to play that season but there was nothing in the ruling that prohibited the Cats from practicing. The late Harry Lancaster, an assistant to Rupp for 26 years, told me that he and Coach Rupp decided to approach the season just as if they were going to play a schedule and that they practiced every day, and they practiced hard. Harry said that Adolph had always been a driven man but that he "was especially fired up that year."

Wildcat fans had to be content that winter to watch four intra-squad games with Cliff Hagan on one team and Frank Ramsey on the other. Gayle Rose, a member of that team, also remembers two games against the professional Minneapolis Lakers in Memorial Coliseum before the start of the season. Gayle recalls that each team won a game and in the Wildcat victory Hagan had a field day. "The Lakers brought in the great George Mikan," Rose said, "And Cliff was really fired up about going against the big 6-10 center. Mikan was considered the best player in pro basketball at the time and even though he was six inches taller than Cliff, Cliff was quicker. He completely outplayed Mikan in that game."

The Southeastern Conference was first to ban Kentucky from league play, but the NCAA followed suit by banning the Wildcats from all collegiate action. Rupp was especially bitter about the NCAA ruling and vowed that he would never retire until the "bastards" who had suspended his team handed him another championship trophy.

Harry Lancaster remembered the final day of practice in that long year off. He and Rupp were sitting in the coaches' dressing room for the last time until the beginning of practice the next fall. Harry recalled that Rupp sat there on a bench in his starched khakis, just staring at the wall in front of him for several minutes before turning to Lancaster with the words, "Harry, by gawd, we're going to make those bastards pay next year."

Memorial Coliseum was wild for that opening game December 5, 1953. The fire marshall must have been looking the other way as every corner was packed and, as the time came for the intro-

Few opponents were able to stop a Cliff Hagan hook shot.

ductions, the crowd was on its feet screaming after every starter's name was announced. Rupp's friend and adversary, Harry Litwack, sat on the bench in the south end zone (yes, the benches were located in the end zones back then) as the starters for the Temple Owls were introduced.

On the bench at the other end of the court, Adolph Rupp, dressed in his trademark brown suit, sat with the Kentucky players. The house lights in Memorial Coliseum were dimmed and a single spotlight was focused right in front of the Kentucky bench. The public address announcer called out the name of one starter, Cliff Hagan.

Cliff was listed as a senior, but actually had received his degree during the suspended season and was in graduate school. The Owensboro native was 6-4 with an impressive physique. Hagan was already an All-American and had led the team in both scoring and rebounding during the 1952 season. Cliff had the sweetest hook shot I've ever seen and he could hit that thing from 15 or 20 feet away from the basket. He also had a great shot from the corner where he could punish opponents who elected to go to a zone. Hagan was a scoring machine but not the greatest defensive player who ever suited up in the blue and white. He once told his teammate Frank Ramsey that, "nobody ever made All-American playing defense."

The next player to step into the spotlight for his introduction was Frank Ramsey. Like Hagan, Frank was already in graduate school and had already been named to the All-American team. Number 30 was 6-3, tall for a guard in those days, but he had great quickness and was a slashing driver when going for the basket. Frank was a very unselfish player and Coach Rupp told me one time, "If we win by 30, Frank might only get you three but if we win by three, Frank will get you 30."

I remember thinking that the name of the third senior would be called next, but instead the announcer called for number 42, Billy Evans, a 6-1 starting forward. He was a junior that season.

Billy was a natural athlete with excellent quickness and was just an outstanding defensive player. He was highly intelligent and could play either forward or guard.

Next to step into the spotlight was Gayle Rose, a six-foot junior guard. Gayle was an outstanding ball handler and a fine passer. He could also hit the outside shot and was very good at starting the offense. He was one of the best dribblers I ever saw but Coach Rupp didn't favor putting the ball on the floor very much.

The introduction of Lou Tsioropoulos completed the starting lineup. Lou was 6-5, the tallest player in the starting lineup. He had been an outstanding football player at Lynn, Massachusetts. Harry Lancaster told me that Lou was actually on his way to Texas for an all-star football game when he stopped off in Lexington for a tryout with the basketball team. They had just painted the floor in Alumni Gym and Harry asked Paul "Bear" Bryant, who was holding spring football practice, to take a look. UK signed Lou on Bryant's recommendation. Tsioropoulos was a very hard-nosed player, just tough as hickory. He was a strong rebounder, and along with Billy Evans, the best defensive player on the team. Lou, like Hagan and Ramsey, was already in graduate school.

Hagan, Ramsey and Tsioropoulos came to be known as "The Big Three" and started every game that season. Rose and Evans were to share starting roles with two sophomores, Linville Puckett and Phil "Cookie" Grawemeyer.

With Kentucky returning to action for the first time in almost two years, emotions were sky-high for that Temple game in 1953. The Owls were expected to be a tough test for the Wildcats but such was not the case. With Hagan setting a Southeastern Conference scoring record with 51 points, the Cats raced to an easy victory, 86-59.

The Wildcats breezed through the first four games on their schedule before the first University of Kentucky Invitational Tournament. Rupp and Athletics Director Bernie Shively had conceived the idea of the tournament and would invite three of the

The 1953-54 Cats posted a perfect 25-0 mark under Rupp, the only time in his 42 years at Kentucky he coached an unbeaten team.

top teams in the country to join the Wildcats. They came with an elite field of Duke, La Salle and UCLA, and Kentucky was up to the challenge, defeating La Salle and the great Tom Gola in the championship game, 73-60. La Salle was to go on that season to win the NCAA Championship.

Kentucky was not only winning, but it was devastating the opposition. The Cats came home from Knoxville with an easy win over Tennessee only to be blind-sided with terrible news. Larry Boeck had written in the *Courier-Journal* that the heart of the Kentucky team, Hagan, Ramsey and Tsioropoulos would not be eligible to play in the NCAA Tournament because they were graduate students. The trio was eligible for the regular season but not for the tournament. UK officials were mad at Boeck, but they should have known of the rule themselves.

It was a big blow, but if it distracted the Wildcats, they didn't show it on the court. That team kept right on rolling and when they laid waste to Alabama on the road, the season was complete. A perfect 24-0.

The SEC was made up of 12 teams then, just as it is now, but the league was divided into thirds. Kentucky was in the division with Tennessee, Vanderbilt and Georgia Tech and played each of those teams twice (at home and away) each season. The Cats would go on the road to play four of the teams while the other four came to Lexington for one game. The SEC ruled that since Kentucky had not played the season before, they would pick up the schedule just as if the Cats had played. Grudgingly, Tulane, Mississippi and Mississippi State agreed to play the Cats in Lexington but Louisiana State flatly refused, contending that since Kentucky hadn't come to Baton Rouge the preceding season, the Cats owed them a visit.

So when the 1954 season ended with both Kentucky and LSU undefeated in conference play, the SEC decreed they would meet in a playoff game at Vanderbilt in Nashville for the league title and the right to represent the SEC in the NCAA Tournament.

Coach Rupp had been experiencing health problems through

much of the season. He had an eye infection during the campaign and had to wear a patch. On the way to Montgomery, Alabama, late in the season to play Auburn, Rupp suffered chest pains and had to see a doctor. He spent much of the week before the game with LSU confined to his home. He and Lancaster made plans to stop LSU and its great star, Bob Pettit. Pettit had led the SEC in scoring for three straight years. He came into the playoff game with Kentucky averaging more than 31 points and 17 rebounds a game. Obviously, stopping Pettit, or at least slowing him down, had to figure uppermost in Rupp's game plan. He decided to play it straight with the guards meeting the LSU guards at midcourt and exerting extreme man-to-man pressure on them. This was an effort to keep the ball out of Pettit's hands. Tsioropoulos, who always drew the defensive assignment on the opponent's best inside player, would take on the big LSU center.

It was an unbelievably warm day for so early in March as Kentucky looked to the playoff game with LSU. It was actually shirt sleeve weather as Harry Lancaster led the players onto the chartered bus in front of the Noel Hotel in downtown Nashville for the ride to Memorial Gym on the Vanderbilt campus and the date with destiny. Coach Rupp was still in his hotel room under a doctor's care after what was described as a mild heart attack earlier in the day. He was ordered to stay in bed all day but Adolph Rupp was one tough human and just before the tip-off here he came, leaning on the arm of Athletics Director Bernie Shively. His instructions to the team were to play tough, hard man-to-man defense, get out on the fast break as often they could and for all five men to crash the boards after every shot because LSU was so much bigger. Then the Cats went to war with LSU and the great Bob Pettit.

A war it was, but Kentucky held a four-point lead, 32-28, at the half. The college game was played in four 10-minute quarters in those days and LSU got it going in the third stanza. The Tigers pulled ahead, 40-36, and Kentucky called a timeout. Shively helped Rupp to his feet and Ramsey told me later that Rupp said,

"By gawd we're beat," but that Lancaster told him to go to a full-court press.

The score was tied at the end of three quarters, 46-46. Hagan and Ramsey began to take over the game and Coach Rupp sent Rose in for Puckett with instructions to "slow it down." What I saw over the next few minutes was something I had not seen all season, nor did I see again over the next 18 years that Rupp was the coach. Rose put on the most awesome dribbling display you could imagine. I mean it was straight out of the Harlem Globetrotters, the best ball handling and dribbling team in basketball.

Coach Rupp despised the dribble and I was shocked to see him send in Rose with instructions to put on a dribbling act just to kill the clock.

"Coach Rupp didn't tell me to dribble," Gayle told me recently. "He just told me to slow the game down but I just did it automatically." Gayle said that when he played for his brother, Jimmy, at Paris, he often put the ball in the deep freeze with his dribbling. He recalled that he once dribbled a whole quarter against Brooksville. Even though Rose's dribbling act saved the day against LSU, he was to go the rest of his career at Kentucky without Coach Rupp giving him the green light to repeat his performance.

When the final horn sounded, Kentucky had beaten LSU by seven, 63-56. Rupp's description of Frank Ramsey being at his best in the big games was right on the money, as Ramsey led all scorers with 30. Hagan scored 17 while Tsioropoulos held Pettit to 17, which was barely more than half his average.

In the dressing room, the Kentucky players were whooping it up. They had given Coach Rupp his first undefeated season, a perfect 25-0. They had won the Southeastern Conference championship and had earned the right to represent the league in the NCAA Tournament. Rupp asked the players if they still wanted to go to the Tournament without the three stars. Ramsey, Hagan and Tsioropoulos argued against it, feeling the team could not win without them and that it would blemish the team's perfect record.

Frank Ramsey (above) teamed with Lou Tsioropoulos and Cliff Hagan to form Kentucky's "Big Three" in the 1953-54 season.

Still, when the vote came, it was 9-3 in favor of going. Nobody ever accused Rupp of running a democracy in his program and he quickly overturned the vote. He informed the team that since Hagan, Ramsey and Tsioropoulos had brought them through the season undefeated the team was not going. Ramsey told me that their coach said, "I'm not going to take a bunch of turds like you to the NCAA."

Gayle Rose recalled that after Rupp's decision he was in the shower when somebody came in to tell him, since the team would not be going to the Tournament, the top players would get their jerseys retired. That took some of the sting out of not going. Seven jerseys that were worn by those players now hang in Rupp Arena, more than from any other team.

When Rupp left the arena, there was a taxi waiting and with Shively still helping the ailing Rupp, the two men left, with a police escort, for the hotel.

After showering and dressing, Hagan, Ramsey and Tsioropoulos decided to head back to the Noel Hotel to check on their coach. Rupp was in bed, but in a talkative mood. The three players asked their coach how he accounted for that fabulous undefeated season and Ramsey said Rupp quickly answered, "Hell, superior coaching."

The 1953-54 team was the only undefeated team in Rupp's 42 years at Kentucky. It was truly a great team, winning by an average of more than 27 points a game. But in a way, it was an unfulfilling season. Rupp had vowed that the people who handed down the suspension would one day hand him the championship trophy. It would come, but the Baron would have to wait another four years.

The Fiddlin' Five

It doesn't matter what Vernon Hatton accomplished as a Kentucky basketball player; his name has become a part of the Wildcat mystique for just one shot in his career.

Never mind that he scored more than a thousand points. Never mind that he was named to the All-American team or led the Wildcats to the NCAA Championship. Vernon Hatton will always be known as the player who hit "The Shot."

"Everywhere I go in Kentucky, people still want to talk about that shot," Vernon said, "and that was back in 1957. It was 48 feet, 10 inches, but it gets longer every year."

The game took place on December 7, 1957, in Memorial Coliseum. Harry Litwack brought in an outstanding Temple team headed by All-American Guy Rodgers. It turned out to be one of the most exciting games in Kentucky's rich history.

The score was tied at regulation's end, and in the first overtime Kentucky trailed by two points with only one second left on the clock. With the ball at midcourt, Rupp signaled for a timeout. Sensing that the cause was hopeless, the crowd began dashing for the exits to get an early start on the traffic. It was during those 60 seconds that the plot was hatched for Hatton's heroics.

"Right before the end of the regulation game, Adrian Smith

was asked to shoot from the outside," Hatton remembered, "and he shot an airball. In the huddle Coach Rupp said, 'Smitty, you've got to try it again, but make it this time.' Assistant Coach Harry Lancaster asked Rupp to let Hatton take the shot. I heard him say that and I said 'Yeah Coach, let me take it.' "

John Crigler took the ball out of bounds at midcourt as Hatton aligned himself with the basket. The pass came to Hatton, and in one motion, he fired a two-handed set shot. The horn sounded while the ball was in the air. It hit nothing but net to send the game into the another overtime. Nothing was decided in the second extra period, as it ended with the score tied at 75.

As the third overtime session played out, the crowd who had left during the timeout before Hatton's shot, began to file back into Memorial Coliseum. The place was packed once again as Kentucky went on to win over Temple, 85-83.

To dismiss the 1957-58 season with Hatton's shot from downtown Lexington would be a mistake. That team was to write one of the real Cinderella stories in UK basketball history.

Pressure was beginning to mount on Adolph Rupp. It had been six years since he had won his third NCAA title, and some in Wildcat land thought the old man had lost his touch. Preseason practice gave Rupp no thought that this Wildcat team might change that. He saw ahead one of the toughest schedules in years. He spoke of what he called a Carnegie Hall schedule and, in his own colorful language, said, "We've got fiddlers; that's all. They're pretty good fiddlers — be right entertaining at a barn dance. But I'll tell you, you need violinists to play at Carnegie Hall. We don't have any violinists."

Rupp had four starters back from a team that had gone 23-5 the season before and made an early exit from the NCAA Tournament. Apparently the press agreed with Rupp that his players weren't violinists. Not one was chosen to the preseason All-American team. But then, 1958 was a true banner year for great college talent. Kansas had Wilt "the Stilt" Chamberlain. Cincinnati had

Vernon Hatton will be remembered for his shot from near midcourt that helped Kentucky knock off Temple in triple overtime.

All smiles here, Adolph Rupp and Johnny Cox were two of the fiercest competitors ever to be associated with Wildcat basketball.

Oscar "The Big O" Robertson. There was the magnificent Jerry West at West Virginia, Elgin Baylor at Seattle, Guy Rodgers at Temple and Tom Hawkins at Notre Dame.

The Kentucky team was led by 6-3 senior guard Vernon Hatton.

Hatton, to me, was one of the greatest clutch players to ever wear the blue and white. He could win games. Vernon was an incredible player when he had the ball in his hands with the game on the line. Harry Lancaster, who was Rupp's assistant on that team, said of Hatton, "If I had to put a man on the free throw line and my life depended on whether he made it or not, Vernon Hatton is the man I'd want to shoot it."

Johnny Cox was the only junior in the starting lineup. He was a 6-4 forward and skinny as a rail. He had the best outside shot on the team and could hook it in with either hand in close to the basket. Johnny was frail, but there has never been a more fierce competitor. Because of his lack of bulk, Cox took a beating, but he was always up to it and actually gave more than he took. John Crigler was the other forward at 6-3. He was a senior, and even though he was not a very good shooter from the perimeter, Crigler was the best driver on the team and was third in scoring behind Hatton and Cox. Crigler had good quickness and was an outstanding defensive player.

Ed Beck was the starting center. The 6-7 senior had the lowest scoring average among the starters, but he was a tremendous rebounder and defensive player. Beck was highly intelligent and seldom made a turnover. He was strong and could really set a screen.

Adrian "Odie" Smith was also a senior, but only in his second year as a Wildcat. He came out of the junior college ranks and was probably intimidated to some extent by the others who had been together for so long. Smith was an excellent outside shooter and usually started the plays from his guard position. He was certainly underrated at Kentucky as he proved through a long and successful career in the NBA. Harry Lancaster said it was the closest-knit team during his 26 years as Rupp's assistant. Vernon Hatton agreed they were close and totally unselfish. "We didn't care who scored. Cox and I usually were the leading scorers but it didn't make any difference," Hatton said. "Everybody was capable of scoring and everybody had a big night during the year. But we

The Fiddlin' Five capped the 1957-58 season by upsetting Seattle, 84-72, to win the national championship.

were role players and everybody knew his role."

In 1958, only 24 teams made it into the NCAA field and for Kentucky to qualify, the Wildcats had to win the last game on their schedule against Tennessee in Knoxville. Kentucky won by 11, outscoring the Volunteers 77-66. Still, UK had lost six games and no team had ever won the NCAA Championship with that many

defeats. Vernon Hatton contends that Kentucky's 19-6 regular-season record was very deceiving. "Only one of our losses came at home, and that was to West Virginia and Jerry West. Half of our six losses, three of them, were by only one point," he says. True. One of those one-point defeats came at the hands of Loyola of Chicago in Chicago. Right at the end of the game the Ramblers got an easy run-out on Kentucky and the shot at the buzzer gave them a 57-56 decision. Rupp was livid.

Back in Lexington the next night on his television show, Rupp told me that his team had not played smart basketball. "We're just not a smart team," he told me. "When they hand out the Phi Beta Kappa keys at the end of the season, I don't think there'll be any dangling from our boys' watch chains."

Still, Kentucky made it to the big dance, and two very fortunate things were in its favor. The fiddlers were playing their sweetest music of the season, and even though they still weren't in Carnegie Hall, it was better. The Wildcats would play the Mideast Regional on their home court in Memorial Coliseum.

The Wildcats were hitting on all cylinders in their first tournament game, burying a good Miami of Ohio team, 94-70.

Despite enjoying a home-court advantage, Kentucky was a decided underdog the next night against Notre Dame. The Irish had one of the premier players in the college game in Tom Hawkins and the night before, against Indiana, Hawkins had ripped the nets for 31 points. Harry Lancaster later remembered that game. "Everyone thought Adolph used the zone defense for the first time in his life several years later," he said, "but we came awfully close to one that night." The UK strategy was to station Beck right behind Hawkins and to drop Smith back in front of the Notre Dame All-American. It worked to perfection. Hawkins scored only 15 points and the Wildcats raced to a surprisingly easy 89-56 win.

The fiddlers only had to travel 80 miles for the Final Four. Louisville's Freedom Hall might not have been Carnegie Hall, but it was the most palatial arena in college basketball. The Wildcats would face their old friends from Temple in the first semifinal.

"Temple had a heck of a team," Hatton told me. "They were highly ranked and they had lost only two games. After we won that triple overtime game, they lost to Cincinnati, who had the great Oscar Robertson. We knew we were in for a tough game."

It was a tough game from start to finish. Nip and tuck. With 24 seconds to play, Temple led 60-59 when Rupp signaled for a time-out. He told the team it would work for a shot from about 10 feet out to be taken by either Hatton or Smith. Beck suggested a diff-

Johnny Cox was the only junior starter on the fabled Fiddlin' Five.

erent play. The UK center felt that Hatton could drive off Beck's screen and that Vernon might get open for a layup. He convinced Rupp it would work. "All right," Rupp told the group, "forget what I told you then and let's go with Beck's play." Hatton remembered that play Beck had recommended. "Ed Beck came out for me and set a screen on my man, and I drove for the basket. I was going to shoot going in but Temple players were all over me. I went on by the basket and flipped it in and there were still about 16 seconds left." Hatton said the team was very concerned, with that much time, that either Rodgers or Temple's outstanding sophomore, Bill "Pickles" Kennedy, would nail a jump shot. Their fears were unfounded. Kennedy bobbled the ball out of bounds and Kentucky held on to win, 61-60.

Rupp allowed his team to watch the first half of the other semifinal between Kansas State and Seattle. Kansas State came to the Final Four favored but, in a hotly contested first half, Seattle led 37-32. Rupp was spared what he would face the next night by his departure with the team during the intermission. Elgin Baylor put on the greatest one-man show I ever saw. He blocked shots. He threw behind the back passes. He just did everything a player could do and he personally destroyed Kansas State, 73-51. If I was impressed, Lancaster and Baldy Gilb, scouting Seattle from press row, were even more in awe of Seattle and the great Baylor.

Lancaster went to Rupp's room after the game to inform his boss that he had no scouting report. "There's no way we can beat them," he told Rupp.

Rupp and Lancaster had failed to come up with a comprehensive game plan when they met with the players at lunch in the Seelbach Hotel. Then came an unexpected miracle.

Rupp later told of the man coming to his room with a plan to beat Seattle. He never revealed the name of the mysterious visitor but after Rupp's death, Lancaster revealed that the mystery man was John Grayson, the coach at Idaho. He brought along a huge roll of film and the advice that was to help the Wildcats spring a

Vernon Hatton scored 30 points in the 1958 NCAA title game to help Rupp win his fourth NCAA championship.

monumental upset. "To beat Seattle," he said, "you must convince your kids that they can't stand there and watch Baylor play. He mesmerizes the other team." Then Grayson started the film and pointed out Baylor had difficulty guarding a player who would drive on him. He felt if Kentucky could get Baylor in foul trouble they could beat Seattle.

"Wake these kids 30 minutes early," Rupp told Lancaster. "We'll give them this new scouting report."

Rupp expected Baylor to guard Beck, UK's low-scoring center. Seattle coach John Castellani had scouted Kentucky in the Temple game and noticed that Crigler had a so-so game. He decided to put Baylor on Crigler. Rupp was surprised and delighted and he ordered Crigler to drive and drive on the Seattle star. Baylor picked up three early fouls, and after he was switched to guard the centers Beck and Don Mills, he picked up his fourth foul trying to guard Mills' hook shot. With Baylor rendered ineffective defensively, Hatton slashed for 30 points, and with Cox's pinpoint accuracy from long range netting him 24 points, the Wildcats dashed to a huge upset, 84-72.

Rupp had won his fourth NCAA Championship. The other three had been no surprise, but it was an unexpected accomplishment for the fiddlers.

At the post-season banquet he said: "These boys are still just a bunch of barnyard fiddlers, but they sure can fiddle!"

Sweeter Than Sugar

Adolph Frederick Rupp could be a man of great charm or a man who could hand out a tongue lashing unequalled in the free world. I doubt that a Kentucky player, during Rupp's 42 years as the coach, escaped the wrath of his temper. Rupp did not confine his anger entirely to his players, and would turn on a member of the media if he disliked something that had been written or said about him or his program. In the 19 years that I was the broadcaster during his career, he read me what he liked to call "the riot act" only once.

Shortly before 6 p.m. on January 14, 1963, the phone rang in the sports department of WHAS in Louisville. The voice on the other end said, "Cawood, this is Adolph Rupp. I'm damned disappointed in you. I heard that you had on your broadcast the news that we were are going to play in the Sugar Bowl Tournament next season. Did you say that?"

I tried to explain that I had simply broken a story that I had discovered on my own but he was having none of that. Rupp insisted I had broken a confidence, that I had betrayed our friendship and that I had embarrassed him by breaking the story prematurely.

Kentucky had beaten LSU in Baton Rouge and had moved on to New Orleans to play Tulane, which was in the Southeastern

Conference then. I ran into Charlie Thornton in the lobby of the Jung Hotel and we went to the coffee shop for some conversation and coffee. Charlie was the Sports Information Director at Tulane at the time and he told me that the Sugar Bowl officials were up in Rupp's room at that moment signing a contract for Kentucky to play in the tournament the next December. Of course, Charlie extracted a promise that his name would not be used if I decided to do the story.

That's what happened, and Coach Rupp was mad as hell. He was never a man to hold a grudge. After he blew his top, the matter was closed. It had long since been forgotten when the team checked into New Orleans, in December, for the 1963 Sugar Bowl Tournament.

Kentucky was going through a recruiting drought in those days, especially recruiting the high-profile out-of-state players. Four native sons started on that 1963-64 team, with Cotton Nash the lone exception. But what an exception.

I first saw Charles "Cotton" Nash in Jeffersonville, Indiana, just across the Ohio River from Louisville. Jeff had one of the best high school teams in Indiana and Cotton was the best player on a team that saw all five starters earn major college scholarships. Cliff Barker, a member of the Kentucky Fabulous Five in the late '40s, was the Jeffersonville coach. Nash was a sophomore on that team and it was to be his one and only varsity season at Jeffersonville. His father, Frank, worked for DuPont and was frequently transferred around the country. After the 1957 season, Frank moved to Texas, and Cotton played his final two seasons across the state line in Lake Charles, Louisiana.

Barker had alerted his two former coaches — Adolph Rupp and Harry Lancaster — that they should keep an eye on Nash as a possible recruit for the Wildcats. "Harry called a lot," Nash said, "and he came to Lake Charles. Coach Rupp also came to see me my senior year. But the biggest pursuer by far was UCLA. I got a call every night from either Coach (John) Wooden or his assistant,

Despite his 6-3 frame, Larry Conley was a great leaper and rebounder for Kentucky in the mid-1960s.

Jerry Norman." Visitations were not limited in those days and UCLA had Nash out to the coast on two occasions. Cotton remembered his second visit. "I had seen a basketball movie, 'Tall Story,' which featured a budding actress named Jane Fonda. I kinda had a crush on her and I mentioned this on my visit. They promised me a date with her if I came to school there." Cotton never did get around to that date because he signed with Kentucky the August after his senior year.

Nash was at Kentucky in an era Harry Lancaster termed the "lean years." The Wildcats were still getting the good home state players but most of the top talent in the other parts of the country was going elsewhere.

The 1963-64 season got underway with Kentucky reeling off eight successive wins. After defeating Notre Dame in Louisville by 20 points, the Wildcats headed for New Orleans and their first Sugar Bowl Tournament in seven years.

Nash was the tallest starter at 6-5. He was a magnificent athlete who had excelled in football and baseball as well as basketball. He was exceptionally small for a center, but he had such great overall skills that he could have played any position on the team. It was his senior season and "King Cotton" had already been named to the All-Conference and All-American teams two years in a row.

Senior Ted Deeken and sophomore Larry Conley were the starting forwards. Each stood just 6-3 and each was frail in stature. Despite lacking height, both players were excellent rebounders. Both were good shooters. Conley had a variety of shots while Deeken specialized in a hook shot. Deeken was from Louisville and Conley called Ashland home. Two other native sons started at guard. Harrodsburg's Terry Mobley operated at one of the backcourt positions while Owensboro's Randy Embry started at the other. Mobley was 6-2 and Embry was 5-11. Both were juniors.

It was one of the shortest starting fives in UK's modern basketball history.

With Nash firing in 28 points, Kentucky easily erased Loyola of

New Orleans on the first night of the Sugar Bowl Tournament to set up a game with Duke for the championship.

The title game was on New Year's Eve, December 31, 1963. The biggest snow storm to hit New Orleans in years fell on the city. Power lines were down. Traffic was slowed to a crawl and there were accidents all over the city. The championship game was delayed for more than an hour to get the lights on in the Loyola Field House. While workers were successful with the lights, the heat system wasn't working and the game was played in a very cold arena. I remember that I did the entire broadcast in my overcoat. Terry Mobley recalled that Coach Rupp told the players to keep their warmups on right up until the start of the game.

Duke was a very large and talented team. Coach Vic Bubas started a pair of 6-10 players inside, Jay Buckley and Hack Tison. Jeff Mullins, a 6-4 guard, was the team's leading scorer. Mullins was from Lexington and Kentucky had waged a determined effort to recruit the hometown product, but Duke won out in the end.

Rupp told his players that, because of the great height advantage the Blue Devils enjoyed, the best chance for the Cats would be to make it a running game and attempt to tire Duke's big men. He also stressed the importance of blocking out in order to compensate for the rebounding edge held by Duke.

All the Kentucky players made major contributions in the game. Conley scored the first four points for the Wildcats and made several steals. Mobley was given the difficult assignment of guarding Mullins, the Duke star. Nash and Deeken, giving away a tremendous height advantage to Duke's pair of 6-10 inside players, would have to play the game of their lives. All of them were up to the task.

The game was close in the early going with the lead changing hands four times. First one team would get a short lead, then the other would move ahead by a few points. After Embry's shot from the corner tied the score at 13-13, Duke began to dominate. The Blue Devils led 47-35 with 10 seconds left in the first half when

*Kentucky won the 1963 Sugar Bowl Tournament title behind the out-
standing play of the event's most valuable player, Cotton Nash.*

Mobley hit his first field goal of the tournament to cut Duke's half-time lead to 10, 47-37.

Mobley said that, in the locker room at halftime, Coach Rupp gave them a good chewing-out before turning it over to Lancaster. "Coach Lancaster told us to feed the ball to Cotton in the second half," Mobley said. "Cotton was having one of his big games. As I recall, he said, 'While we may not be able to guard their two big kids, it's for darn sure they sure as heck can't guard Cotton.' So we went out in the second half to run our plays in an effort to get the ball in Cotton's hands."

The Cats began to slowly chip away at the Duke lead and with 7:07 to play, Nash hit a long jump shot to tie the score at 70. Deeken was having a big second half for the Cats and his hook shot pushed Kentucky in front for the first time since early in the game, 72-70.

Buckley hit one of two free throws to cut the Kentucky lead to one, and when the Cats got the rebound, they called timeout with exactly five minutes remaining. Kentucky worked the ball to Deeken, and again he hit a short hook shot to push the Cats ahead, 74-71. Buckley returned the favor at the other end to cut the margin to one, 74-73. Nash, playing one of his greatest games as a Wildcat, outmaneuvered the big Duke front line for a layup. That gave him 30 points for the game and gave Kentucky a 76-73 lead. Tison scored for Duke to make it 76-75. Embry's free throw with 3:41 remaining in the game made it 77-75.

Now it was Duke's turn to rally. Each of the Duke giants, Buckley and Tison, made a close-in field goal to push the Blue Devils ahead by two, 79-77. Only 1:38 remained. Terry Mobley was about to have a game that he would remember the rest of his life.

Larry Conley had fouled out midway through the second half and another sophomore, Tommy Kron, had come on to take his place. Two years later, the two would be the heart of a great Kentucky team called "Rupp's Runts." Kron wasn't waiting for that. He got his chance in that Sugar Bowl Tournament and turned in an excellent performance. He was assigned to guard Mullins and really shut him down toward the end of the game.

With the Cats trailing Duke 79-77, Kentucky got a fast break going. Kron was bringing it down the middle of the floor and saw Mobley running the right wing. He got Terry the ball and Mobley hit a 12-foot jump shot to knot the count 79-79. There was still 1:29 left to play.

Duke called timeout with 59 seconds to go, and Bubas told his team to work the ball around for a good shot, getting it into the hands of Mullins, Tison or Buckley. Perhaps the Blue Devils were being too cautious. Deeken slapped the ball out of the hands of Duke's Tison and Kron grabbed the loose ball. There were 47 seconds left in the game. Kentucky called a timeout.

"Coach Rupp designed this play that would get me the ball," Nash recalled recently. "I was having a good game and everybody in the gym knew I would take the last shot. When we went back out, Duke put three men on me and there was no way I could get the ball."

Embry and Kron were more successful at killing the clock than Duke had been, and they worked the clock down to 12 seconds before passing the ball to Mobley who would feed it into Nash. "Everybody knew we were going to Cotton," Mobley said. "They were sagging all over him and time was running out. I had no choice but to shoot the ball, and fortunately it went in." Terry was about 15 feet out and slightly to the right of the key. The shot hit the board and banked into the net and Kentucky had beaten Duke, 81-79. Was Mobley the designated shooter? "Oh, hell no," he laughed.

The crowd in Loyola Field House was a very partisan Kentucky crowd and the fans flowed onto the floor to celebrate a remarkable Kentucky win. Nash had scored 58 points in the two-day event and was named the MVP for the Tournament. Oddly, he almost didn't play in it.

Nash's family had moved to Massachusetts, as his father had

Randy Embry's excellent guard play helped the Cats to a 21-6 record during the 1963-64 season.

been transferred again. Frank Nash had taken a week of vacation to drive to Louisville for the Notre Dame game and then on to New Orleans for the Sugar Bowl. He brought along Cotton's mother and sister. The players could get as many as four tickets for family and Nash went to Rupp's room to collect his.

"I went to Coach Rupp and told him I wanted my family tickets," Nash said. "He told me he didn't have any. I told him the tickets were for my mother, father and sister, who had driven all the way from Massachusetts. He insisted he didn't have any tickets. It really rubbed me the wrong way and I said if they couldn't go to the game, I wasn't going either. I told him I'd just take them to a movie."

Nash insists he was serious about not playing. How was the confrontation resolved? "I went back to my room," he remembered, "and about two hours later, Harry Lancaster knocked on my door. He looked at me real sternly and handed me the tickets. He turned and left without saying a word. I never again mentioned the tickets to the coaches and they never mentioned them to me."

Nash was MVP, but Mobley was the star of the game with his shot that made the difference. He remembered that, among all the hoopla and celebration after the game, Rupp walked up to him to congratulate him. "He put his arm around my shoulder and said, 'That play worked didn't it, buddy?' I said, 'Yes sir it did.' He said, 'Just between you and me, everybody knew the ball was going to Cotton and I told you to shoot.' I said, 'Yes sir.' " Terry said that as they walked off the floor Coach Rupp said, "That's our story and we're going to stick to it."

Mobley said he remembered reading in the New Orleans papers the next day that Coach Rupp had anticipated Duke's sagging defense on Nash and had told Mobley to take the shot. "In reality," Terry laughed, "I just couldn't get Cotton the ball."

Nash said that winning the Sugar Bowl Tournament trophy was exciting, but that the players were more excited later that week when the polls came out and Kentucky was ranked No. 1 in the

Rupp had many occasions to smile as Larry Conley and his teammates captured the 1964 SEC championship.

country. "It had been years since Kentucky had been No. 1," he said, "and we were proud to get the program finally back where it belonged."

Kentucky went on to win the Southeastern Conference championship, but bombed out in the 1964 NCAA Tournament.

Duke had the last laugh. The Blue Devils made it to the final game of the NCAA Tournament before losing to UCLA. It was the first of 10 national championships for John Wooden.

Revenge Against the Hoosiers

A basketball play-by-play announcer, so I'm told, should not get emotionally involved with the team he is covering. I've never bought into that theory. I have always believed that if a person followed one team over a number of years and didn't care whether it won or lost, that person was in the wrong line of work. For 39 years, I felt the pain when the Cats lost and the thrill of watching them win.

December 7, 1974, was a very painful night. After two wins to start the season, the Cats headed to Bloomington for their annual date with Indiana. Kentucky not only lost to the Hoosiers, Kentucky was embarrassed. As we rode out of town, I remember sitting there in the car thinking, "This is going to be a long winter."

This was the senior year for a group of players Joe B. Hall had recruited. As a freshman team, they had gone 22-0 and been dubbed the "Super Kittens." Kevin Grevey, Jimmy Dan Conner, Mike Flynn and Bob Guyette were starters as seniors. During their junior year, they posted a 13-13 record, the worst in Hall's 13 years as the Kentucky head coach.

In 1974, as seniors, the former "Super Kittens" were joined by another great recruiting class of Jack Givens, Mike Phillips, Rick Robey and James Lee. A rules change now allowed freshmen to

Kent Benson of Indiana (left) grounded Kentucky center Mike Phillips to help the Hoosiers to a 98-74 early-season win.

Coach Joe B. Hall had reason to be down after the initial meeting between the Wildcats and Hoosiers during the 1974-75 season.

compete on the varsity and Robey moved into the starting lineup with Conner, Flynn, Grevey and Guyette.

Grevey was a 6-5 forward who moved into the starting lineup as a sophomore, the first year he was eligible to join the varsity. He was a smooth mover who played with great finesse. He was one of Kentucky's best medium-range shooters with that sweet left-handed stroke. Kevin was very outgoing and a very likeable young man. He was regarded the best player in Ohio coming out of high school and he got better with age as a Wildcat.

Conner was "Mr. Basketball" in Kentucky as a high school player, and he too, joined the starting lineup as a sophomore. Jimmy Dan was a very tough competitor. He's the guy you'd like to have as a foxhole buddy. He was the leader on the team as a senior and he really was at his best in the big games. He was a tough defensive player who could dominate an opponent.

Mike Flynn, like Grevey and Conner, became a starter as a sophomore. Mike had been "Mr. Basketball" in the state of Indiana and came to the Wildcats with impressive credentials. Flynn was the quickest of the Cats and also an outstanding defensive player. He could really pick an opponent's pocket. Mike was a good scorer, but with so much firepower on that team he was content to be more of a playmaker and defensive specialist.

Guyette moved into the starting lineup as a junior. At 6-8, he was the tallest of the former "Super Kittens." Bob had played the center position his junior year and was a good scorer and a rugged rebounder. With the addition of Robey and Phillips, Guyette was moved to a forward position opposite Grevey. Robey, at 6-10, gave the Cats much-needed height.

That was the lineup Hall sent against a very talented Indiana team Bob Knight had assembled in Bloomington for that December 7 engagement. Hoosier center Kent Benson totally dominated Robey. He outscored, outrebounded and physically dominated the Kentucky freshman. It wasn't just Robey who was abused. The Hoosiers totally dominated Kentucky and coasted to a 98-74 blowout. It could have been worse, but Knight called off the dogs and sent his subs in with several minutes to play. The game was even more lopsided than the score would indicate.

Two nights later in Louisville, the Wildcats seemed destined to revert to their losing ways of the year before when they played a good North Carolina team. The Tar Heels had almost doubled the score at 31-16 when Hall called a timeout. He benched four starters. When the starters got back into the game, they went to war. Leading the charge was Conner, who scorched the nets for 35 points to lead the Cats to a 90-78 victory over a fine North Carolina team. Hall called it Conner's best game ever. Grevey said recently "Jimmy Dan was our emotional leader. When we started to sag, he would do something spectacular to bring us back up. He would pop us in the chest and say, 'Come on, we gotta win. Let's play.' I don't think I ever saw a player just take over a game the way

Benson and his Indiana teammates found the going much rougher against Kentucky's "Slaughterhouse Five" in the teams' second meeting.

he did against North Carolina." Grevey said the North Carolina game put the team back on track to have a good season.

The team lost only four more games the rest of the campaign and won a share of the Southeastern Conference championship and made the NCAA Tournament.

Kentucky had an easy time against Al McGuire's Marquette team with a 76-54 win at Tuscaloosa, Alabama, to advance to the Mideast Regional in Dayton, Ohio. The Wildcats dispatched Central Michigan to make it into the regional final against their old adversary, Indiana.

The Hoosiers hadn't just flexed their muscles against Kentucky. They had raced through their entire schedule undefeated with an average win margin of 23 points. They came into Dayton that afternoon ranked No. 1 in the country and were favored by a dozen points over the Wildcats.

The UK players were actually looking forward to the rematch. Hall had told them they would have to meet Indiana's physical play with a physical game of their own. Grevey said every player realized he would have to be at the top of his game for the entire 40 minutes to beat Indiana and all the players were really excited that afternoon. "Mike Flynn wanted it in the worst way," Grevey said. "Being from Indiana, I know it really meant a lot to him."

The Hoosiers opened up as if it was going to be a second straight rout of the Wildcats. They dashed out to an 8-2 early lead and led by seven before Kentucky caught up at the half, 44-44. The first half had been very physical, but the second half was almost like a brawl with each team dishing it out. Flynn had played magnificently in the first half, but he really turned his game up a notch after the intermission. He went a perfect six-for-six from the field and led Kentucky with 22 points. Kent Benson was brilliant again with 33 points and 23 rebounds, but he couldn't overcome the overall play of the Wildcats and Kentucky prevailed, 92-90, in one of the best games anybody ever saw.

Kentucky held the 92-90 lead with only five seconds to play. The

A more rugged Phillips helped Kentucky avenge its prior loss to the Hoosiers with a 92-90 win over Indiana in the NCAA Tournament, despite another stellar performance from Benson.

Cats lined up in single file right in front of our broadcast spot for an inbounds play and I caught Grevey's eye. He just puffed out his cheeks and went, "Phew!" as if to indicate just what a tense, tough game it had been. Conner got the inbounds pass, but by the time Indiana chased him down to foul him, only one second remained. Conner missed the free throw, but the game ended before Indiana could even try a shot.

A Chicago sportswriter dubbed that Kentucky team the "Slaughterhouse Five." He wrote they were like five guys who make their living sledge-hammering steers in a stockyard. It was a brutally physical game, make no mistake about that. Grevey looked back at the game and said, "It was the most physical game I ever played in, bar none, and I played 10 years in the NBA. I can't remember a game I played in at Kentucky that was as important or where we had more at stake. After being annihilated by Indiana in Bloomington earlier in the season, we seniors really wanted our last year to be special and we realized one way to do that was to beat Indiana in the rematch."

I followed the team bus from Dayton back to Lexington. As soon as the bus hit the state line, a police escort picked up the team. Memorial Coliseum was packed when the players arrived and they had the damnedest celebration you ever saw. You would have thought the Wildcats had already won the national championship. The win over Indiana meant that much — perhaps too much.

Grevey said the Wildcat players celebrated for two days before going to the Final Four in San Diego. "It was the biggest win in our careers at Kentucky," Grevey said. "I think we all thought that beating No. 1 ranked Indiana was our championship. We spent ourselves, no question about it. If Goose Givens hadn't had such a great game against Syracuse, we might have struggled with that team in the semifinal."

Kentucky romped past Syracuse, but lost two nights later to UCLA in John Wooden's last game as the coach of the dynastic

Indiana native Mike Flynn took great pleasure in cutting down the nets after the Wildcats beat Indiana to earn a trip to the 1975 Final Four.

Bruins. UCLA won a scrappy 92-85 decision for its 10th NCAA championship.

Kentucky fans everywhere remember the win over Indiana that season, and it still ranks as one of the greatest NCAA Tournament games ever played. The Chicago sportswriter who dubbed Kentucky the "Slaughterhouse Five" called the Wildcats' win their biggest in a decade. Kentucky fans would call it one of the biggest in history. After the Final Four, Kentucky was met with another big celebration back in Lexington and Joe B. Hall got an extension on his contract.

Going Out in a Blaze of Glory

If ever a team enjoyed a better home-court advantage than the Wildcats did in Memorial Coliseum, it has been a well-kept secret.

When the 11,500-seat facility was completed in 1950, at a cost of almost $4 million, many skeptics were quick to brand it a "white elephant." It never was. Memorial Coliseum was a success right from the start — both on the court and in the stands. When the Wildcats moved to Rupp Arena in 1976, Kentucky teams had lost only 38 times while recording 308 victories. No win came any harder than the last one.

Coach Joe B. Hall was understandably nervous for the final game scheduled in the Coliseum as he prepared to close out the season against Mississippi State on March 8, 1976. He had lost the guts of the team that had made it all the way to the NCAA final the year before. Kevin Grevey, Jimmy Dan Conner, Mike Flynn and Bob Guyette had graduated. Rick Robey, who had started as a freshman, was injured at mid-season and was out for the year.

"I had invited Coach Rupp and Harry Lancaster to sit on the bench with us that night," Hall said, "and we had a lot of former players back who had played in that first game in the Coliseum. It was a rebuilding year for us. We were 10 and 10, but we had won five in a row going into that game with Mississippi State."

An overflow crowd of around 13,000 packed in for the final Wildcat
game in Memorial Coliseum on March 8, 1976.

Hall liked his team's chances of winning but he was a bit more on edge than usual knowing it would be the Wildcats' last game in the Coliseum.

It was a very emotional night. A crowd estimated at 13,000, 1,500 over capacity, came early and came ready. The old place was

rocking and had reached a frenzy when the ceremonies began. There was Rupp, decked out in his traditional brown suit, on the bench. Reggie Warford, the team's only senior, came out to a standing ovation. The night was off to a perfect start.

The Wildcats went ahead early but Mississippi State caught up and seemed to be in control as the half ended with the Bulldogs on top 50-42.

They maintained that lead as things began to go badly for Kentucky. The Cats had to play the last six minutes without their big man when 6-10 Mike Phillips was ejected from the game for committing, what the official perceived as, a flagrant foul. Mike had scored 22 points and hauled down nine rebounds.

"It was a terrible call," Hall remembered. "State's Al Perry had fallen down and he just locked his legs around Mike's legs. All Mike did was just try to get loose. The official claimed Mike kicked Perry. It was a very bad call and it cost us our only big man."

When 6-5 James Lee fouled out a little later, Kentucky was really reduced to a small lineup. Jack Givens, at 6-4 was the tallest Kentucky player on the court. He was joined by Merion Haskins, Bob Fowler, Larry Johnson and Reggie Warford.

With only 83 seconds showing on the clock, Mississippi State was leading 84-77. Surely there was no way the Cats could pull this one out. Surely they would suffer the indignity of losing the last game ever played at Memorial Coliseum. During a timeout, some of the Mississippi State players walked over to their radio announcer to shout to the folks back home that the Bulldogs had beaten Kentucky. There was much celebration. The celebration turned out to be a bit premature.

"We were so doggone small we didn't have any business beating anybody," Hall said. "I told our players that we were quicker than they were and that if we would really hustle on defense, we could still win the game. Merion Haskins came up with a big steal for us and that really got us going."

Johnson drilled a 15-foot jump shot. After another steal, Warford hit from the baseline and Kentucky had cut four off that seven-point lead as the scoreboard showed the Bulldogs still in front, 84-81.

Perry went to the free throw line for a one-and-a-bonus. He hit the first but missed the bonus, and Kentucky got the rebound that resulted in a Johnson layup at the other end. State led 85-83 and only 43 seconds remained. The Bulldogs were showing signs of folding. They were making turnovers and hurrying their shots.

James Lee waged war with the Bulldogs' inside operatives all night long before fouling out in regulation.

Kentucky outscored the Bulldogs eight to one in the final 83 seconds to send the game into overtime.

State was trying to run off some clock, and Kentucky had to gamble on a steal. The Bulldogs' Ray White was fouled. He went to the line but missed the first shot of a one-and-one. Kentucky got the rebound and called timeout with only 26 seconds left.

Remember, there was no three-point shot back in 1976. The Wildcats best hope was to score a field goal and send the game into overtime.

"We set up a play during the timeout," Hall said. "We had plenty of time to get a good shot and we called a play that would get the ball to [Bob] Fowler, in close to the basket."

Fowler broke for the basket too early, rendering the play useless. Givens still had the ball and was trying to ad lib a play. All of a sudden he found himself wide open. "The only thing I could do was shoot it," Givens said. Shoot he did. Score he did. The incredible comeback was complete. Kentucky had outscored Mississippi State eight to one over the last 83 seconds. The score was tied 85-85 but the game would be decided in overtime.

"Our little team just hung in there," Hall said, "and we felt that we had all the momentum on our side." In the overtime, Givens scored inside and Johnson hit from outside to get the Cats off and running. Mississippi State had to foul and Kentucky made five of eight free throws down the stretch. The Cats pushed the lead out to 94-91 and Joe B. told his players not to foul. State ran down court for an uncontested basket and Kentucky had earned a wild and crazy 94-93 victory.

"All the Kentucky tradition, all the history and all the spirits of past players won that game," Hall told me recently, "I really believe that," he said.

Hall awarded the game ball to his old boss and predecessor, and Rupp seemed to be in the best mood anyone had seen since he was forced out as the coach four years earlier.

It was a happy crowd that saw the Cats go out a winner at Memorial Coliseum, the house that "Rupp built." But it was an exhausted bunch of Wildcat supporters. I remember, after doing the postgame program with Joe, I was walking back out onto the floor of the Coliseum and I saw this lady still sitting there. "I don't know whether we'll renew our season tickets next year or not," she told me. "This team has just about killed me. I liked it better in the old days when you could just sit back and watch them kill somebody." Let the record show she was right back in Rupp Arena backing the Cats the next season.

That Kentucky team went on to the NIT when that entire tournament was still played in New York and still held much more stature than it does today. Kentucky was one of several fine teams in the field. Joe B. again invited Coach Rupp to accompany the team to New York.

"Blowout" was a foreign word to that Kentucky team. It had to play hard to win close decisions. First up for the Wildcats was Niagara. Kentucky led most of the way but Niagara kept coming back on the Cats. Behind a 20-point, eight-rebound performance by James Lee, the Cats earned a 67-61 decision. That gave the Cats the right to move on to face one of the seeded teams in the tournament, Kansas State, with its talented backcourt tandem of Chuckie Williams and Mike Evans.

"Kansas State was one of the favorites to win the tournament," Hall recalled, "and we knew we had to play a super game to win."

It was another struggle but with Lee again having a 20-point game, the Cats prevailed 81-78. Providence had upset Louisville, another seeded team, to set up the semifinal game.

I always admired the coaching abilities of Joe B. and he really put on a coaching clinic in the NIT that year. He had a different game plan for every team the Wildcats faced and each plan worked to perfection. Providence had a big center, Bob Misevicius, who was very mobile in the open court. Against Louisville, Misevicius took the Cardinals' center in backcourt and just drove by him all day. Mike Phillips was a fine center but Mike wasn't the quickest player who ever lived. Hall devised a plan where James Lee would guard Misevicius in the backcourt and there wasn't a center in the college game who could drive by Lee in the open court. If Misevicius went down inside, Phillips picked him up.

Kentucky led most of the game, but a fine Providence team kept battling back and finally gained the lead at 78-77 with just

Jack Givens' jumper tied the Mississippi State game at 85 to close out regulation. He also hit the first basket in the overtime period to get the Wildcats started, and they went on to post a 94-93 win.

seven seconds showing on the clock. The Cats called a timeout.

"James Lee had the hot hand that whole tournament," Hall said, "and I told Larry Johnson to look for James down low."

Coach Joe B. Hall presented the game ball to Adolph Rupp following the final Kentucky victory in the "House That Rupp Built."

Phillips bobbled the inbounds pass but got control and passed to Johnson. Larry didn't have time to look for Lee, so he took it to the basket himself. He twisted under for the shot among a host of Providence defenders and it went in. Kentucky won 79-78.

Kentucky had won its first three games in the NIT by a total of 10 points. The Cats had beaten Niagara by six, Kansas State by three and Providence by one. The Wildcats now would face North Carolina Charlotte for the championship. The 49ers, like Kentucky, had been squeaking by all of their opponents. UNC Charlotte was coached by a native of Lexington, Lee Rose, who had built a fine coaching reputation at Transylvania. At UNC Charlotte, Rose had a good team led by a marvelous player named Cedric "Cornbread" Maxwell.

Fouls plagued the Wildcats in that title game. With more than 10 minutes to play, Givens, Phillips and Lee were all on the bench with four fouls. Reggie Warford, the only senior and the team captain, had not scored a field goal in Kentucky's first three NIT games but he got it going when he had to. He nailed 14 points in the championship game, and it was his jump shot that pushed Kentucky ahead for good at 64-63. The Wildcats went on to win the big trophy with a 71-67 decision.

"That team was the most fun to coach of any team I had at Kentucky," Hall told me recently. "We didn't have much size and we didn't have much experience, but they were a scrappy bunch. That team was very close. Any coach likes to see his team improve as the season goes along and that team was only 10-10 at one point in the season. It won its last 10 in a row for a 20-10 record and an NIT championship."

That team did accomplish a lot, including closing Memorial Coliseum with an impossible comeback victory. It just kept rolling from there. It seldom won by much but, somehow, it usually found a way to win.

The Fabulous 14

Alexander Gomelsky is a small man with gray hair and while his name might not have been a household word in Kentucky in early November, 1977, he was well known among the men who coached basketball all over the world. Gomelsky coached the Soviet Union National Team and brought them into Memorial Coliseum to meet the Wildcats. After watching Kentucky virtually destroy his team 109-75, Alexander, in his broken English said of the UK team, "Best team I ever look."

This was Joe B. Hall's sixth team after he took over the coaching duties from Adolph Rupp. Hall had won or shared three Southeastern Conference Championships, a National Invitation Tournament and had gone on to the final of the NCAA Championship in 1975 before losing to UCLA in John Wooden's last game. Still, he was unable to escape the long shadow of the legendary Rupp. Hall had what he considered to be his best team for the 1977-78 season and even before the campaign got underway, he told the Lexington Rotary Club that his goal was to win the NCAA championship.

Joe B. had good reason for his optimism, since had a veteran team returning. Most of the players had been there the year before when the Wildcats ran off a sparkling 26-4 record and ad-

The basketball world lost a great teacher on December 10, 1977, when Adolph Rupp passed away.

vanced to the NCAA Regional Final before losing to North Carolina by seven. The entire front line was back, which included the "Twin Towers," Rick Robey and Mike Phillips, along with Jack Givens. All three were seniors. Truman Claytor, a junior, was at one of the guards, while Kyle Macy was the newcomer to the starting five at the other guard.

Robey was 6-10 and strong as a bull. He was the most outgoing

of the Kentucky players and was certainly one of the leaders on the club. He was the most seasoned player on a veteran team. All the seniors had been battle-tested as freshmen when Kentucky went to the Final Four, but Rick was the only one who started most of the games. He was the leading rebounder and second-leading scorer on the 1978 team.

Phillips was also 6-10 and, like Robey, had the power and strength to have his way around the basket. He was very accurate in his field goal attempts, especially when he got the ball in the low post. Mike was a very aggressive player and never backed down from anything.

At 6-4, Jack "Goose" Givens was the smallest of the front court players, but he was a ballet dancer in sneakers. Givens was so smooth another of his nicknames was "Silk." He was a talented left hander who could really light it up when he hit his groove.

Jay Shidler likely would have been one of the starters but he broke his foot during preseason practice and actually showed up for media day on crutches. Truman Claytor took over for him in the backcourt. Claytor was a much underrated player on that team. He could bust a zone with his excellent outside shooting and he played a good hard-nosed defense.

Coach Joe B. Hall had maintained during the off season that Kyle Macy would make the big difference in the team. Macy had transferred after his freshman year at Purdue and had been red-shirted the previous season. Kyle's father was a coach, so Macy was one of those gym rats who really understood the game. He was an excellent shooter from the perimeter and was at his best when the game was on the line. He still holds several Kentucky free throw shooting records.

If there was a better sixth man in the country than James Lee, his name is a secret. Lee was 6-5 with an imposing physique. Macy said players on the other teams would often ask him if the senior was as mean as he looked. Lee actually was somewhat of a cutup off the floor, but he had the ability to completely turn a game around when he came in off the bench.

Hall had a long and talented bench. Shidler, Freddie Cowan, Dwane Casey and LaVon Williams had many great moments for the Wildcats during the season.

The talent and experience of that 1978 team was not lost on the pollsters. Kentucky was everybody's No. 1 at the start of the season. The Cats lived up to the billing. They opened up with homecourt wins over Southern Methodist and Indiana and went to Lawrence, Kansas, to take on a talented Jayhawk team. Kentucky won a hard-fought 73-66 decision, but that will always be one of the saddest days in Kentucky basketball to me. It was December 10, 1977. We left Allen Fieldhouse after the broadcast on a night that seemed extremely cold compared to our weather back in Kentucky. Back at the motel, I went by the room of Jim Payne and Seth Hancock. It was there that I got the devastating news. Adolph Rupp was dead. Seth had called back to Kentucky and learned of the death. I knew that Coach Rupp was very seriously ill, but to me, he just seemed indestructible. During my first 19 years of broadcasting the Kentucky games, Rupp had been the coach. He was my friend, my mentor, just a person I admired tremendously. The news of his death was a great blow.

The team was playing up to its No. 1 ranking. It ran off 14 straight wins before a trip on January 23, 1978, to Tuscaloosa, Alabama. C.M. Newton's Alabama team belted the Cats 78-62.

Newton recalled that game recently. He said that his assistant, Wimp Sanderson, came back from scouting UK with the word that Alabama simply couldn't match up with Kentucky. Newton had a fine team led by Reggie King who was to become the leading scorer in Alabama history. "Since Wimp felt we couldn't match up with Kentucky's tremendous advantage in size," Newton said, "we thought we might give them some matchup problems by starting a smaller, quicker team. We started three guards and it worked out well for us."

Kentucky came back home to win three straight against Georgia, Florida and Auburn before heading back out on the road to play LSU. It was to be the most dismal trip of the season. Dale Brown had a good team led by two Kentuckians, Rudy Macklin and Kenny Higgs. If losing wasn't embarrassing enough for Kentucky, the way it lost was. With the game tied at the end of regulation play, all five LSU starters had fouled out going into the overtime. LSU won 95-94.

Because of Kentucky's size and strength, opposing coaches had some unflattering things to say about the Cats. Kentucky was brutalizing the game. Kentucky had taken the finesse out of the game. But the unkindest cut of all was to come from the coach. Some of

Jack Givens rose to the occasion in the NCAA final against Duke, as the Goose scorched the nets for 41 points.

Kentucky's best teams had nicknames such as the "Fabulous Five" and the "Fiddlin' Five" but a disgruntled Joe B. Hall, after the game, suggested this group should be known as the "Foldin' Five."

Kentucky slowly began to right its ship after the LSU debacle and went undefeated through the regular season and put another SEC Championship in its trophy case.

The run for the NCAA Championship began in Knoxville against Florida State. Hall fretted that most upsets come in opening games in the NCAA and he turned out to be almost a prophet. The Seminoles outplayed the favored Wildcats and held a 39-32 lead at the half. Hall was so angry with his starters that he went to his bench for the start of the second half with Dwane Casey, LaVon Williams and Fred Cowan starting in place of Robey, Givens and Claytor. They joined Macy and Phillips for the second half tip-off and that makeshift lineup actually cut two points off the Florida State lead. When Hall came back with the starters, UK won a hard-fought 85-76 decision. Macy said, "We had been lucky. We had won on a bad day."

The Wildcats moved on to Dayton, Ohio, for the Mideast Regional, to face Miami of Ohio. It was no contest, as Kentucky's size and experience was too much for Miami, and the Wildcats coasted to a 91-69 victory.

That set up the Regional Final with Michigan State and its fabulous freshman, Earvin "Magic" Johnson. The Spartans' coach, Jud Heathcote, seemed concerned with Kentucky's size and muscle. Before the game, Heathcote said, "Even watching Kentucky kind of bruises you up a bit." He packed in a zone to stop the Cats' powerful inside game and Michigan State held a 27-22 lead at the half. That was an outstanding Kentucky team because it could adjust to almost any situation, and it was a suggestion from Hall's assistant, Leonard Hamilton, that caused Hall to improvise in the second half. As Kyle Macy recalled, "We had already left the dressing room and were warming up for the second half when Coach Hall yelled for Rick Robey and me to come over to the bench.

While we were standing there, he went over this play for us." Hall went over the plan that Hamilton had suggested. Robey would come out high around the top of the free throw circle and set picks for Macy. That forced the Spartans to let Macy stroke the jumper or to foul him. It worked to perfection. As Macy remembered, "With a little over six minutes to play, Rick set a perfect pick on Michigan State's Terry Donnelly and I hit my jump shot off the right side of the free throw circle. Donnelly got me just as I shot and I made the free throw." That broke a 41-41 tie and Kentucky went on to win 52-49 and earn a trip to the Final Four in St. Louis.

In the semifinal in the Checkerdome, Kentucky faced an Arkansas team led by three guards — Sidney Moncrief, Marvin Delph and Ron Brewer — and coached by Eddie Sutton, who would become Hall's successor at Kentucky in 1985. The game was billed as Kentucky's power against the quickness of Arkansas.

It was an outstanding game with Kentucky clinging to a 32-30 lead at the half. The Cats began to take control in the second half after Sutton went to a zone to protect his team, which was in severe foul trouble. When that didn't work, he went back to man-to-man, even going into a full-court press, and cut the Kentucky lead to one. Macy thought a play Hall had put in earlier that season was the key to a Kentucky victory. "I thought our 'Rick Rick' was the key play," he said. Against the press, Macy would take the ball out of bounds, Robey and Phillips would station themselves at midcourt and Claytor and Givens would try to get open for the inbounds pass. If that didn't work, Macy would yell, "Rick Rick," and Robey and Phillips would run toward Macy to get open while Givens would wheel and head for the Kentucky basket on a dead run. Against Arkansas, Givens got open for easy layups and Kentucky went on to a narrow 64-59 win.

All season long, Kentucky had been painted as a big, muscular team without quickness. It was not an accurate description. Robey had good quickness for his size and Givens and Claytor had good quickness by any comparison. After the loss to the Wildcats, Sut-

James Lee's emphatic dunk put the finishing touches on a 94-88 Wild-cat win over Duke to give Joe B. Hall his national title.

ton said as much: "Anybody who said Kentucky did not have quickness should have his head examined." Duke coach Bill Foster, after watching Kentucky beat Arkansas, said, "Kentucky has been represented as a power team because of their big frontcourt players, but I'm impressed with their quickness and their pressure defense." Two days later, Foster would send his Duke team against the Wildcats for the national championship.

Sunday was an off day for the teams to get in their final practices and to attend the obligatory press conferences. The stories that came out of those painted Duke as a young, fun-loving team and Kentucky as a sober, too-serious bunch. Jack Givens said the team went to St. Louis for only one purpose. That purpose was to win the championship.

Macy gave much of the credit for that team's success to the leadership of the four seniors. He said when the team went back to the dressing room following warmups that, before the coaches got there, the seniors reminded the other players to remember all the things the team had gone through and how close the team was to its goal. When Coach Hall went over the game plan, he reminded the team that Duke had used the fast break to get to the final and he wanted them to shut it down and not to allow any runouts. Macy said, "I don't think they got a single one on us."

Duke opened in a 2-3 zone, and as the game unfolded, Hall noticed they were packing the inside players back deep while using the front two to guard against the outside shooting skills of Macy and Claytor. Hall noticed that left a hole right in the middle of the zone. He recalled after the game, "When we saw how open Duke was leaving the middle, we junked our game plan and just tried to get it to Jack."

If any Kentucky player had a more spectacular game than Jack Givens did in that 1978 NCAA final game, I can't dig it out of my memory bank. He was magnificent. Not that he was a one-man show; he wasn't. Robey took 11 shots and hit eight. Macy fired only three times from the field and made them all. This was a very un-

Rick Robey, who had an outstanding shooting night himself, savored the moment after the nets came down in St. Louis' Checkerdome following the Wildcats' victory to claim the 1978 national championship.

selfish team, and with Givens holding the hot hand, his teammates got him the ball. The smooth lefthander put it up 27 times, almost 40 percent of the shots taken by the whole team. Givens had saved his best for his last game as a Wildcat, and his 41 points shredded the Blue Devils.

Hall took his starters out late in the game, but as Duke closed the gap, the starters went back in and won the game, 94-88. James Lee running out on the final UK play to put the icing on the cake with one of his patented thunder dunks.

It was the fifth NCAA Championship for the Wildcats. It was a shining hour for Joe B. Hall, recognized now for the fine coaching it took to build and develop the team and to guide it through the perilous waters all the way to the title. He had finally escaped the foreboding shadow of Rupp. It was a shame Rupp didn't live long enough to see Hall and the Wildcats win. He would have been very proud.

The Kentucky cheerleaders linked arms out in the center of the court there in the Checkerdome and their words expressed the feelings of Kentucky fans everywhere, "The sun shines bright on my old Kentucky home..."

Nobody was calling these champions the "Foldin' Five." Not now. The team never did pick up one of those nicknames Kentucky fans like to bestow. Make no mistake this was a TEAM and I liked a homemade sign a fan held aloft at the celebration the next night in Memorial Coliseum. It read "The Fabulous 14."

Kyle and Claytor and the Boys

In my 39 years as the UK basketball announcer, I could count on one hand the times I thought the situation was hopeless for the Wildcats near the end of the game. Certainly one of those games took place during the 1978-79 season. Remember, there was no three-point shot then and Kentucky was trailing by six points with only 31 seconds to play. I saw no chance for the Cats. Could you blame me? Well, that night I learned my lesson.

Kentucky won the NCAA Championship in 1978, but when Joe B. Hall marshalled his troops for the start of the 1978-79 season, the heart and soul of that championship team was gone. Rick Robey, Mike Phillips, Jack Givens and James Lee had played out their eligibility. Both starting guards, Kyle Macy and Truman Claytor, were back, as were experienced players Jay Shidler, LaVon Williams, Fred Cowan and Chuck Aleksinas. Added to the mix was a talented freshman class of Dwight Anderson, Chuck Verderber and Clarence Tillman.

For the opening of the season, Hall started Aleksinas at center, Williams and Verderber at the forwards and Macy and Claytor at the guards. After coasting past La Salle and West Texas in Rupp Arena, the Cats eagerly anticipated a visit from the Kansas Jayhawks. Kansas had won all four starts and had two of the premier

A familiar sight during the 1978-79 season, Truman Claytor heading up the court after forcing a turnover.

players in the game in Darnell Valentine and 7-2 Paul Mokeski.

Dwight Anderson had worked his way into the Kentucky starting lineup, replacing Verderber at one of the forwards. The Dayton freshman was only 6-3, but he could really jump and move. I thought he was the quickest player to ever suit up in the blue and white and I gave him the nickname "The Blur."

Kentucky got its first lead over Kansas early in the game, as the Cats edged ahead 10-8, but from there on it was all Kansas and the Jayhawks led by 10 at the intermission. Kentucky kept fighting back and, with Macy and Shidler connecting from long range, the Wildcats cut it to two points inside the last three minutes. Macy, known more for his shooting than his defense, made a clean steal from the dribbling Tony Guy and raced down the court for a layup to tie the count at 56-56 with 2:43 left in the game. Kansas was playing for the last shot, but Claytor put such defensive heat on Valentine that the officials called for a jump ball with 52 seconds left. Kansas got the tip and called a timeout with 19 seconds left to set up the last shot. Everybody in Rupp Arena knew it would be taken by Valentine. It was, but the shot was off target at the buzzer. Overtime. The Jayhawks took command again in the overtime and that brought us to the situation where Kentucky was down 66-60 with only 31 seconds to play. During a timeout, Coach Hall recalls that he had not lost hope. "Actually, I still thought we would win the game. I told our players exactly what we had to do to win. We had to draw a charge and we had to make some steals." That was about to happen.

Kansas coach Ted Owens had cautioned his team against fouling and Anderson was able to drive unmolested to the basket to cut the lead to four, 66-62. Only 22 seconds remained.

Kansas took the ball out of bounds and the Kentucky players put on a ferocious defense. Before the ball ever was put in play, Valentine was called for pushing Anderson and the Kentucky player was put on the free throw line. Unfortunately, Anderson missed. Fortunately, in a wild scramble for the rebound, Anderson used his quickness to come up with the ball. As he drove for the basket, Mokeski was called for the foul. This time, with only 10 seconds left, "The Blur" hit both free throws. Kansas 66, UK 64.

The fur was really flying. Kansas called its final timeout.

Coach Hall gave the team virtually the same instructions he had given earlier — try for a steal or hope for a charging foul; if that didn't work, foul. Hoo boy, what a game!

On the inbounds pass Anderson again called on his incredible quickness and was able to deflect the ball. It was clearly going out of bounds, but Anderson left his feet and made just an impossible play. With his back to the court, soaring through the air, he tipped the ball back onto the playing surface with one hand. It was the last he saw of the play as he went tumbling head-over-heels into the UK bench.

Kyle Macy didn't see the defensive acrobatics of Anderson. Macy was face-guarding his man, trying to deny the inbounds pass. When he heard the roar of the crowd, Kyle turned to see what was happening. What he saw was the ball bouncing his way. Macy scooped it up and moved toward the basket. From 15 feet away, he squared up and let it fly. Swish! Three seconds left. The scoreboard beamed the incredible comeback: Kansas 66, Kentucky 66.

Kansas' John Stallcup instinctively signaled for a timeout, but the Jayhawks had already used up their allotment and a technical was called.

Macy was at the line. He got one shot. The game was now his to win. As he did so many times during his career, Macy won it. True, the ball bounced a few times on the rim, which was very unusual for a Macy free throw, but the ball dipped into the net and Kentucky had completed a remarkable comeback to win 67-66.

By no means was the 1978-79 Kentucky team one of the top Wildcat units and after that heart-stopping win over Kansas, the Cats dropped two of their next three. Still, the Cats took a 4-2 record to Louisville to face the nation's second-ranked team, Notre Dame. Leading by 12 points in the second half, coach Digger Phelps, for some reason, changed his defense, putting pressure on the UK guards in a man-to-man situation, while putting his three big men inside in a triangle zone. Hall made a brilliant counter-move, by placing Anderson in the top of the key. He was

Kyle Macy earned most valuable player honors following a stellar SEC Tournament in 1979, which included a 32-point outburst by the sharp-shooter against Ole Miss in the opening round.

far too quick for Notre Dame's big people and ran around and through them the remainder of the game as Kentucky won, 81-76. Anderson won the Bernie Shively Trophy, which went to the best player on either team for their annual game.

The wheels fell off as Kentucky opened Southeastern Conference play and the Cats won only one of their first six games. As so often happens during bad times, UK lost a starter when Chuck

Aleksinas quit the team. Kentucky won several close games at the end of the season but still was able to finish no better than 16-10. The regular season was over but the Southeastern Conference Tournament was being revived after a 27-year absence.

This was a young Kentucky team with only two seniors, Truman Claytor and Dwane Casey. Claytor was a hard-nosed player who always was assigned the other team's best offensive guard. His teammates called him "T.C." and he was very popular with the other players. Claytor had a tendency to be a streak shooter but when he had his stroke, he could be devastating from long range.

No player ever worked harder than Casey. He probably saw less playing time as a senior than he did during his junior season but he was always ready when Joe B. sent him into a game. Dwane worked just as hard in practice as he did during a game and he took the off-season so seriously, he built himself to the point where he was the strongest player on the team.

For the renewal of the SEC Tournament in 1979, they came up with a strange format. The two top-seeded teams, LSU and Tennessee, were required to win only two games to win the championship while all the other teams would have to win four games to capture the title.

Kentucky's first opponent was Ole Miss. The Cats had beaten the Rebels twice during the regular season, and with Macy shooting the lights out in the third match, the Wildcats won 82-77. Kyle's 32 points was his best scoring effort as a Wildcat. The Cats advanced to the second round to face Alabama.

Claytor and Jay Shidler had been sharing the guard position opposite Macy for most of the season, but in Kentucky's strong showing at the end of the season, Shidler had gained the starting spot. Just minutes before the game with Alabama tipped off, Joe B. decided to start Claytor.

"It's just a feeling I think every coach gets in his gut from time to time," Hall said. "I can't tell you why but I thought Truman was ready to give us a big game." Did he ever!

Claytor, one of just two seniors on Joe B. Hall's team, helped Kentucky reach the final of the first SEC Tournament since 1952.

C.M. Newton did not have one of his powerhouses at Alabama, but he still had a couple of outstanding players in Reggie "Mule" King and Robert Scott. It was not a great Kentucky team either, but Hall did have a pair of great shooting guards in Macy and Claytor.

It was an intensely played game right from the opening tip. First one team would go on a run, then the other would answer with a run of its own. With the Crimson Tide leading 7-6, Kentucky scored eight unanswered points to move on top 14-7. Later an Alabama run pushed the Tide in front 19-18. And so it went throughout the first half until the Tide got hot and mounted an eight-point lead, 55-47, with 16 seconds left in the half. A Macy jump shot just ahead of the buzzer made it Alabama 55, Kentucky 49, as the first half ended.

Claytor and Alabama's King put on a shooting clinic in the second half. King scored 18 of his 38 points and Claytor poured in 21 of his 25 after the intermission. Truman, in fact, was unstoppable over the final 20 minutes, going a perfect nine for nine.

Nobody threw in the towel during this hectic game and with 52 seconds to play, Kentucky held a one-point lead, 99-98. Alabama had the ball and with 30 seconds to go the Tide called a timeout.

King had fouled out a minute earlier and Newton really had only one choice. Robert Scott was having a hell of a game. He had taken 11 shots and connected on 10 of them. Newton, like all good coaches, tabbed Scott to take the last shot. C.M. told his team to work the clock down to eight seconds and the Tide would win or lose on Scott's final heave.

With 10 seconds left on the clock, Scott began to make his move to take Macy one-on-one. Anderson realized what was happening and left his man to help Kyle. Macy got a hand on the ball as Scott pivoted to his left and Anderson ran to the ball to make the steal. Scott, in his frustration, fouled Anderson and Dwight went to the line for the one and the bonus. He nailed both and put the game out of reach at 101-98. Kentucky elected not to guard Alabama, and without the three-point shot all Alabama's Joe Hancock could do was go for the layup. Final score: Kentucky 101, Alabama 100.

In the game, Kentucky and Alabama combined to set two SEC Tournament records — most points in a single game and most points by both teams.

The Wildcats also set a school field-goal accuracy record by shooting a torrid 68.3 percent. Next, the Cats would face the reg-

ular-season champion LSU team which would be playing in the tournament for the first time. It would be the third game in three days for Kentucky.

It's funny how we can remember some things. I remember that the Kentucky-LSU game was only 23 seconds old when Dwight Anderson broke his wrist and was lost to the team. The reason I recall the time so vividly is that Anderson wore No. 23.

The other players just went at it harder and with Macy scoring 29 points and Claytor adding 20, the Cats won surprisingly easy, 80-67. Kentucky had been the biggest surprise of the tournament and now would face Tennessee for the championship.

Tennessee was well rested. It was only the second game of the tournament for the Vols, while Kentucky was playing for the fourth time in four days. Kentucky was noticeably tired but still managed to tough out a lead by halftime.

With a little over two minutes to play in the game, the score was tied at 55-55. Kentucky went into a stall until it called timeout with 12 seconds left to set up the last shot. Coach Hall told Macy to try and rub his defensive man off on a screen and to take the last shot. Tennessee's Terry Crosby got through the screen. Macy faked and Crosby left his feet. Kyle went up for the shot and the two players brushed. There was no foul call and the shot missed. The ball came right back to Macy. Realizing there couldn't be much time left, Macy hurriedly pushed the ball back up. Again it was off target. The game went to overtime and the Vols won 75-69.

Macy was the tournament's high scorer with 93 points and was named MVP. Claytor joined him on the all-tournament team.

The season actually ended back in Rupp Arena. The Cats were invited to the NIT and faced Clemson on UK's home court. Clemson won in overtime, 68-67.

Kentucky finished the year with 19 wins and 12 losses, not a good record by Kentucky standards, but that was one of the most enjoyable seasons I spent with the Wildcats.

A Christmas to Remember, A March to Forget

Kentucky was loaded for the 1983-84 season. The latest edition of the "Twin Towers" was made up of seven-footer Sam Bowie and 6-11 Melvin Turpin. Joining these two seniors in the frontcourt was a marvelous sophomore named Kenny Walker. The starters in the backcourt were seniors Jim Master and Dicky Beal. Master was a deadly outside shooter and Beal was quick as a cat. The Cats had a strong bench with Winston Bennett, Roger Harden, James Blackmon and Paul Andrews.

Kentucky opened the season at home with an easy 65-44 win over Louisville. After plugging out a 24-11 victory over a stalling Cincinnati team in the Queen City, the Cats took a perfect 6-0 record on the road to play Illinois on Christmas Eve. It was the only time the Wildcats played on the day before Christmas in all of my 39 years as the UK broadcaster, and it is a trip I'll never forget.

Kentucky was originally scheduled to play the Fighting Illini in late December, but when the Illinois football team made it to the Rose Bowl, school officials asked Kentucky to change the date.

"It was going to be an afternoon game," coach Joe B. Hall remembered. "I talked with the players, and since we would get home early that evening, they were all for playing on Christmas Eve. Lou Henson, the Illinois coach, was a good friend and we were glad to help him out."

The weatherman took care of the schedule. When Kentucky's chartered DC-3 landed at Champaign, it was greeted by a huge snow and bitter cold. The high temperature for the day was a minus five degrees. Wind and blowing snow combined to make the wind chill read a minus 65.

The Wildcats made it to the arena for the game, but the officials weren't as fortunate. Three spectators with refereeing experience were drafted out of the stands and given whistles and sneakers.

Illinois was a perfect 8-0. A Bowie dunk and a 15-footer by the lanky senior got Kentucky off and running. But Illinois seemed to seize the momentum and, by halftime, was ahead 33-26. The Cats seemed headed for overtime after having to scratch and claw to stay even for the first 39 minutes and 52 seconds. That's when Hall signaled for a timeout with eight seconds left and the score tied 54-54. The Cats brought the ball across midcourt before calling the timeout.

Hall asked James Blackmon to check into the lineup and during the conversation on the sideline, Joe told the team they were going to run a one-on-one for James. In Kentucky's first few games that season Blackmon had been sensational, but was in a typical freshman slump before the Illinois game.

"I just had a gut feeling that James was the player to take the last shot," Hall remembered. "We had run the same play for him against Indiana, and his basket sealed the win for us." The ball came in to Blackmon and his teammates backed down near the baseline setting up a one-four offense. Blackmon was to take his man, Bruce Douglas, and try to beat him one-on-one. James moved just to the right of the free throw circle but Douglas was right in his face. Blackmon rose for a 15-footer and his shot appeared to be just off to the right but it hit the glass and banked in as the final second ticked off the clock. Kentucky won 56-54. The 7,000 fans who had braved the bitter cold and deep snow gave both teams a standing ovation.

Kenny Walker's inside moves were the perfect complement to the power games of Melvin Turpin and Sam Bowie for the 1983-84 Wildcats.

Both coaches, Hall and Henson, gave the makeshift officiating crew high marks for their work. Joe B. says it was the only time in his coaching career that an official came to him after the game to ask for his autograph.

Despite the horrid weather conditions, some of the players left right after the game to join their families for the holidays. Blackmon, who was from Indiana, was one of them and he missed sharing his moment of glory with the media in the post-game press conference. Some of the other players had made plans to leave for home after the plane got back to Lexington around 6 p.m.

Earlier that day, Hall received a call that, because of the extreme cold, they were unable to start the team plane but that a heater was being flown in from Chicago and the plane should be able to depart on time. It was after the game that Joe discovered that Chicago's O'Hare Airport had also been closed and that the repairs could not be made on the plane. Hall would have to find another way to get his team back to Lexington. He isn't exactly sure now how he did it.

"I know we called Greyhound and some of the other established bus lines," he laughed, "but none of them had anything available on such short notice on Christmas Eve. I don't remember exactly how we found out about him, but we learned of a man there in town that owned and operated his bus and we were able to get him to agree to drive us to Lexington."

No one who made that trip will ever forget it. The heating equipment on the bus simply could not compete with the sub-zero night. It was cold on the bus, so we all sat with our overcoats pulled tightly around us. The defroster fought a losing battle and Hall and Leonard Hamilton took turns standing by the driver to wipe away the frost from the inside of the windshield. The diesel fuel was turning to jelly and the bus labored up the steeper inclines at about 15 miles per hour. I sat with Dr. Otis Singletary, the UK President, and I wondered why the big chief himself would make such a journey on Christmas Eve. "I couldn't find anybody at the uni-

Sam Bowie helped Kentucky tip Indiana early in the season, 59-54.

*In a game that featured two of the biggest big men — Akeem
Olajuwon and Melvin Turpin — Kentucky came out on top, 74-67.*

versity other than the players or coaches, who was going," he said, "so I thought somebody ought to represent the school." Dr. Singletary told me that he was going to invite any of the players who couldn't get home to come to his home for Christmas dinner.

While Santa was making his rounds all over the world, the UK traveling party was making its miserable way to Lexington. The bus pulled in front of Bluegrass Airport at about 6 a.m. on Christmas Day. Everybody agreed it was a horrendous journey, but to Joe B., the trip was worth it. "James made my Christmas," Hall said.

If the Illinois trip was disconcerting to the players, it certainly didn't show in their play. The Wildcats ran off five more wins to push their record to 12-0. The Cats finished the campaign with 23 wins against only four losses and claimed another Southeastern Conference championship.

Kentucky had been dominant in the SEC Tournament in the early days, winning 13 of the first 19 championships before the tourney was discontinued after 1952. After the tournament was resumed in 1979, the Wildcats failed to win for five straight years. Many UK fans blamed the very unlikely string of losses on Hall, an outspoken opponent of the tournament since its revival. "I was against it because I think it was renewed for all the wrong reasons," Hall said. "There wasn't that much interest in it outside of Kentucky and Tennessee, and I thought it took too much out of a team that was going on to the NCAA. But anybody who thought I didn't want to win every game I played just didn't know me very well." Hall's 1983-84 team was to get the monkey off his back.

The SEC Tournament was held in Vanderbilt's Memorial Gym in Nashville. First up for the Cats was Georgia, and with Melvin Turpin putting on a clinic, the Wildcats coasted to a 92-79 win. Turp equaled the scoring record for a tournament game when he fired in 42 points, matching the record set 32 years earlier by another Wildcat, Cliff Hagan. That would be Kentucky's only laugher in the tournament. Against Alabama the next night, Hall went to a play that had won at least two games for him that season. He

When it comes to aerial acrobatics, few Wildcats have matched the exploits of Kenny "Sky" Walker.

sent his team to a 1-4 offense, but this time it was Dicky Beal who was to take his man one-on-one. Beal came through and the Cats moved into the final with a 48-46 win over the Crimson Tide.

Even though Kentucky had won the regular season championship, more than a few gave Auburn the edge to win the tournament title. Each of the two teams had won a lopsided victory on its home court. Auburn boasted two All-SEC players in Chuck Person and Player of the Year Charles Barkley.

"I knew they were good players," Hall recalled, "but I didn't know they were such great players until I saw what they did in the NBA." Both teams went at each other with a vengeance. The game was 40 minutes of nail-biting, with neither team able to gain much of an upper hand. There was a stretch in the second half where, on 11 straight trips downcourt, the offense scored and the lead changed hands on each occasion.

With Auburn leading 49-47, the Cats got a break when the Tigers turned the ball over. Kentucky ran some time off the clock and waited for a play to develop. Sam Bowie rolled to the basket and Beal lobbed the pass toward the hoop. Bowie took it in the air and slammed it through, completing a perfect alley-oop play to tie the score at 49-49. It was another Auburn miscue that gave Kentucky the ball for the last shot. The Tigers' Gerald White had the ball and when his teammate, Person, faked UK's Kenny Walker out of his shoes and broke for the basket, White rifled the pass. Kentucky's Winston Bennett anticipated the pass and broke in front of Person to make the interception.

Surely Joe B. would call for the old one-on-one that had been so successful for him that season. "We had won with that the night before against Alabama," Hall said, "and I thought Sonny (Smith the Auburn coach) would be looking for it. Kenny Walker hadn't hit a thing in that Alabama game (one for 11) but he was filling it up in the Auburn game. We wanted to get the ball in Beal's hands to start the play and Turpin and Master would set a double screen for Kenny."

Well, you know what they say about the best-laid plans. Auburn had seen Beal beat the Crimson Tide and the Tigers weren't about to let history repeat itself. With only 14 seconds left on the clock and the score tied at 49-49, Auburn assigned its fine guard, Paul Daniels, to get in Beal's face and stay there. Dicky just couldn't get open to take the inbounds pass. Master, sensing that his roommate was in trouble, broke out and took over Beal's role. In one of the greatest ad-lib plays ever, Beal realized that Master had become the playmaker, so he dropped down to help Turpin set the double screen. Walker broke out around the screen and Master hit him with the pass. Kenny took a couple of dribbles and went up for a 15-footer just to the right of the free throw circle. The ball was short and it hit the front of the rim. The ball bounced high in the air, hung suspended, and then dropped through the net as the final horn sounded. Kentucky won, 51-49.

The Kentucky players began a wild celebration after winning their first SEC Tournament since its revival five years earlier. The Auburn players were devastated. Charles Barkley just sat down on the court and cried like a baby.

The Wildcats became the first team to win the regular season and tournament championships in the same year since the SEC started the tournament again in 1979. They took their sparkling 26-4 record to Birmingham and trounced Brigham Young in the NCAA Tournament to earn the right to return to Rupp Arena, where the Mideast Regional was being held.

First up for the Wildcats was their in-state neighbor, the Louisville Cardinals.

After UK and U of L had not played for 25 years, Louisville won an NCAA Tournament overtime decision in March 1983. The Cats opened the 1983-84 campaign with an easy win over Louisville, but the Cards showed a lot of improvement in the rematch.

Beal and Bennett gave Kentucky its final push and UK prevailed, 72-67. Then the Cats earned Hall his third trip to the Final Four by outlasting Illinois, 54-51, in the regional title game.

Legendary tough guy Charles Barkley could only sit and weep after Kenny Walker's jump shot dropped through the net to give Kentucky a 51-49 victory in the 1984 SEC Tournament title game.

This was Kentucky's second close win over the Illini during the same season but this time coach Lou Henson was irate, complaining bitterly about the officiating. I have always felt that his tirade

Sam Bowie had many an alley-oop dunk in his career, and will be remembered as one of the most mobile big men in Wildcat history.

had a lot to do with the NCAA later changing the rule so that no team could play an NCAA game on its home court.

What happened in Seattle at the Final Four is still impossible for me to explain. It was the most colossal collapse of a Kentucky team that I ever saw. The Cats faced Georgetown and its intimidating center, Patrick Ewing, in the national semifinal in the Kingdome. Kentucky turned in a sterling first half and took a seven-point lead to the dressing room. Then came a total fold-up as the Cats took 33 shots and made only three in the second half. Georgetown won 53-40. Unfortunately, that left a bitter aftertaste on what had otherwise been a brilliant season.

The Year College Basketball Changed Forever

The news came out of Kansas City like a bolt from the sky. In late summer of 1986, the NCAA Rules Committee dropped a bombshell on the nation's college coaches that would change the game for the coming season and for all time to come. There had scarcely been a hint that the Committee was coming out with the rule that any shot taken from behind a line positioned 19 feet and nine inches from the basket would count for three points. Shock waves rumbled through every campus in the country.

"It did catch all of us by surprise," said Eddie Sutton, who was the coach at Kentucky at the time. "If we had had any idea the rule was coming, it would have affected our recruiting plans. One or two good shooters that we didn't take would have been high on our list."

Still, Sutton believed he had players who could shoot the three. "We felt that James Blackmon and Ed Davender would be able to shoot the three and with Rex Chapman and Derrick Miller coming in, we thought both of them would be able to score from behind the arc."

Sutton had several players returning from the 1985-86 team that had fashioned a spectacular 32-4 record, had won both the SEC regular season and Tournament championships. They had advanced to the NCAA Elite Eight before losing a two-point decision to LSU, a team the Wildcats had beaten three times that season. All-American Kenny Walker and playmaker Roger Harden

Prior to the 1986-87 season, a change in NCAA rules instituted the three-point basket, which paved the way for "3-mania" that is now commonplace in Rupp Arena.

were gone, but in addition to Blackmon and Davender, Sutton was counting on veterans Winston Bennett, Cedric Jenkins, Paul Andrews and Rob Lock. Not long after the beginning of practice however, Bennett went down with a knee injury that would sideline him for the season and Jenkins suffered a stress fracture that put him out of action for half the season.

Right from the start of practice, Sutton began working on the three-point shot. "Yeah, we sure did," he said. His optimism about his shooters was confirmed. Blackmon, Davender, Chapman and Miller were all accurate from behind the arc. "A lot of people think I'm conservative, but I'm not. If I've got somebody that can shoot the basketball, I'm going to turn him loose," Sutton said. "I gave those players a green light to shoot the three."

If any player ever came to Kentucky with the fanfare that preceded Rex Chapman, it's lost to history. The 6-5 guard, one of the most recruited players in years, came out of Apollo High School in Owensboro, Kentucky. He had been named to the High School All-American team two years in a row. The Associated Press named him Male Athlete of the Year in Kentucky and he was chosen as the state's "Mr. Basketball."

It was a day for celebrating when Chapman cast his lot with UK. "Our assistant coaches did a good job recruiting Rex," Sutton said, "but I think he always wanted to come to Kentucky." The press worked overtime with slogans like Rex the Boy King, and John McGill, then a sports columnist for the *Lexington Herald-Leader*, suggested the name of the city should be changed to "Rexington."

Chapman didn't start the first game that season against Austin Peay, but with Kentucky trailing, Sutton sent Rex into the game almost eight minutes into the contest. He scored 18 as Kentucky came back to win and Chapman remained in the starting lineup for the rest of his career.

Sutton, who always liked a three-guard lineup, finally settled on Chapman, Davender and Blackmon at the guard spots and Richard Madison and Rob Lock inside as his starters. That group

Derrick Miller's outside shooting skills made him a big fan, and user, of the three-point shot.

won five of its first six games, dropping a five-point decision to Indiana, as it moved to Freedom Hall for the much anticipated meeting with the Louisville Cardinals.

Whether taking it inside or firing from the perimeter, James Blackmon enjoyed a productive senior season on offense.

Louisville had won the NCAA Championship the prior season and still had the tournament's MVP, Pervis Ellison, when the two teams squared off on December 27, 1986. The Cardinals had lost some key players from that championship team and Kentucky looked to be a bit stronger. The Louisville fans were ready. Sutton had flamed the fire earlier in the season by referring to U of L as "little brother."

"I'll never make that mistake again," he laughed recently, "but I didn't mean for it to sound condescending. I was thinking Kentucky had the longer tradition, but boy did I get the Cardinal fans upset."

Sutton thought Kentucky was a slightly better team than the Cardinals that season, but he expected it to be a close game. He worked long and hard against the Louisville press and, with Freedom Hall packed to the rafters, the game began. No one expected what was about to transpire. Kentucky had really embraced the three-point shot and by the time Davender, Chapman and Blackmon had all hit from behind the arc, the Cats had moved ahead 12-10 and they were on top to stay. Three of UK's first four baskets were from three-point territory. The middle one, a rainbow from behind the NBA line by Chapman, seemed to signal that the Cats were on their game. With Rex leading the way, the Cats had moved ahead by 10 at the intermission, 38-28. Chapman had scored 18 of Kentucky's points, including three three-pointers and a leaning, off-balance shot just before the first half ended.

In the UK dressing room, Sutton told his troops not to let up in the second half. He counted on a UK lead keeping the crowd out of the game. He needn't have worried.

The Cats ran off the first 10 points of the second half and outscored Louisville 22-4, on the strength of three more three-pointers. The Cats led 60-32 with 11:30 left in the game.

Sutton remembers that game well. "I thought we were a little better than Louisville that year," he says, "but I sat there in shock like everybody else. I sure didn't expect to see anything like what I was watching." What he was watching was Kentucky exploding for an 85-51 victory, the worst defeat in Denny Crum's career.

Chapman was brilliant from outside, scoring 26 points, which

Ed Davender was part of a big Kentucky comeback that helped it knock off Tennessee 91-84 to avenge a Wildcat loss in Knoxville earlier in the 1986-87 season.

included five three-pointers. Surprisingly, the Wildcats also dominated the inside with Madison hauling in 17 rebounds and Lock outscoring and outrebounding Louisville's Ellison. It was two dunks by Lock that ended that incredible game. Sutton said,

"Everything just went our way." What an understatement!

The Louisville game was the zenith of the entire season for Kentucky. They went on the road to lose to Georgia in the very next game and managed only an 18-9 regular season record. Still, there were certainly some exciting moments during that campaign. At Alabama, Kentucky met the team that had beaten it by 14 points in Rupp Arena. Down by six points with 1:23 remaining, the Cats clawed back and Davender's shot with six seconds left gave the Kentucky a 70-69 win. The next game against Tennessee even outdid that one.

The Vols had beaten Kentucky in Knoxville earlier that season and the Cats clearly had revenge on their minds for the rematch in Rupp. The first half was a see-saw battle that saw first one team on top and then the other. With three minutes left in the half, the Vols were on top 31-29 but Kentucky ran off 10 unanswered points to take a 39-31 lead to the dressing room.

Kentucky had held Tennessee's Tony White (the leading scorer in the SEC) to only four points in the first half. But White caught fire after the intermission and blistered the nets for 16 second-half points. He led the Vols back. With only 1:13 remaining in the game, Tennessee was on top by 10, 75-65. It looked hopeless. The Kentucky faithful lost faith and began filing out of the arena. To be honest, had I not been hooked to a microphone, I would have been tempted to join them. Sutton had not lost the faith.

"I've been around the game of basketball long enough to understand that anything can happen," he said. "With the way the three-point shot had come into the game, you've always got a chance to pull it out at the end." Sutton encouraged his players to believe they could win.

Kentucky fought back. Chapman fired in a three-pointer from 22 feet. Tennessee 75, UK 68. Next, Rex got the chance from the charity stripe and converted two free throws to cut it to 75-70. But when White went to the stripe and made a pair for the Volunteers, he pushed the Tennessee lead back to seven, 77-70. There were

Rex Chapman, the prototypical long-range bomber, had 26 points and made five three-pointers in the Wildcats' 85-51 pasting of Louisville.

only 44 seconds to play. More of the Wildcat faithful headed for the exits. The last glimmer of hope seemed to be gone.

Irv Thomas took a turn at being the hero when he grabbed a missed shot and put the rebound into the hoop. Tennessee 77, Kentucky 72. The scoreboard clock showed 35 seconds remaining.

Kentucky still had a chance but would need some help from the enemy. The Vols' Doug Roth provided some help when he missed the front end of a one-and-the-bonus. Kentucky got the rebound and Davender brought the ball downcourt and pulled up for a gutsy jump shot from 21 feet. Swish. The Vol lead was now down to two, 77-75. Only 12 seconds remained. "I knew we had to foul and to foul quickly," Sutton said. "We would liked to have the time to foul their worst free throw shooter but with so little time left, we just had to foul whoever had the ball."

Unfortunately, the ball came in to Dyron Nix, one of Tennessee's best free throw shooters. Nix would get the one-and-the-bonus. Only 11 seconds remained on the clock and Kentucky called a timeout.

"Tennessee was missing free throws and showing signs of tensing up," Sutton said. "We wanted to try and ice Nix with the time-out, and as soon as the timeout was over, we turned right around and called another one. I told our players that if he missed the front end of a one-plus, I wanted to just go for a two-pointer to tie and I wanted Rex or James or Ed to take the last shot."

As the teams broke huddle and headed for the Tennessee free throw line, the students and the diehards really raised the roof, trying to rattle Nix. Ed Davender was so sure that Nix would miss, he told Chapman to take the last shot. Davender related to Rex that it was his turn since Davender had hit the game-winner just a few days earlier at Alabama.

The pressure was squarely on Nix. If he made the first shot, Kentucky would have to hit a three to send the game into overtime. If he made both ends of the one-and-one, the game was almost surely out of Kentucky's reach.

Nix had connected on six of his seven charity tosses as he toed the line for his most important free throw of the game. He missed. Richard Madison pulled down the rebound for UK and fed it out to Chapman who began his coast-to-coast dash to glory. Doug Roth, a 6-11 sophomore center for the Vols, moved out to pick up Chapman. Rex faded to his left and put up a soft 12-footer that

Ed Davender helped Kentucky close out the 1986-87 regular season with a 75-74 win over the Oklahoma Sooners.

The Benchmark Game

I think it was the late Paul "Bear" Bryant who first came up with the opinion that a tie was like kissing your sister. The accomplished coach was describing his frustration on the outcome of a football game when neither team won or lost but broke even in the contest. Following a college basketball team that breaks even over the course of a season isn't exactly a barrel of fun. Not usually. Adolph Rupp's 1967 team posted a 13-13 record after finishing second in the nation the previous season and Joe B. Hall's 1974 team who posted the same record after winning the SEC Championship the prior year, left UK fans frustrated and disappointed. Yet Rick Pitino's 1990 team that went 14-14 caused great rejoicing in Wildcat land.

Following severe NCAA penalties and the transfer of the best UK players, Pitino was left with only eight scholarship players from which to rebuild the down-trodden UK program. While flying across the Atlantic after the trip to Italy in the summer of 1995, I asked Rick how he approached that season. "I just wanted to put in our style of play that I thought would be beneficial down the road. I didn't think in terms of winning and losing. I was thinking of the future of the team. I thought our up-tempo style would be fun for the fans and interesting to the players we would be re-

Reggie Hanson, all 6-7 of him, held his own against a much taller LSU frontline and helped the Cats pull off the improbable upset.

cruiting. I thought that would be enough for the first year."

Pitino put in an excruciating conditioning program but, by the time his preseason practice sessions ended, he realized that seven players would have to carry the banner for the Wildcats. "I didn't think you could play the style of play that we play with so few players. They were going to have to play so many minutes," he said.

Pitino's debut as the Kentucky coach saw the Wildcats squeak out a 76-73 win over Ohio U. in Rupp Arena. He took the Cats to Indianapolis and played a good Indiana team right down to the wire before losing 71-69. "I thought then," he said, "that we could be a competitive team despite a lot of short-comings." The low point of the season came at Kansas where the Jayhawks ran wild against the Wildcats, winning 150-95, the worst loss in modern history for a Kentucky team. Back at home, Kentucky played heavily favored Louisville on even terms before losing by seven.

As conference play began, the Cats were winning at home but losing on the road. Still, they were 12-10 — already with more wins than anyone had predicted — when Dale Brown brought a fine LSU team to Lexington for a rematch with the Wildcats.

LSU won the first game that season, down in Baton Rouge in easy fashion and his Tigers were heavily favored to make it two in a row over the Cats. LSU was ranked No. 9 in the nation, was leading the SEC and had won seven straight games heading into the game at Rupp Arena. Even though LSU had coasted to a 94-81 victory in Baton Rouge, there were plenty of fireworks in that game. Pitino and Brown almost came to blows at one point. Both downplayed the incident after the game, but I was there and I really thought the two coaches were going to start swinging. The SEC office was so concerned that it made a change in the officiating crew for the second game. The veteran Don Rutledge was brought in for Paul Andrzejewski, but the game was played without incident.

The LSU game was to be the biggest of the season for Pitino's first edition of Wildcats. A record crowd of 24,301 yelled itself hoarse even before the opening tip-off. Jerseys in honor of former

UK coaches Adolph Rupp and Joe B. Hall were unveiled in a ceremony before the game. Two former Wildcat greats, Dan Issel and Cotton Nash, were introduced to the crowd. Wild hysteria was rampant in Rupp. Kentucky was a decided underdog.

"I've never believed in moral victories," Pitino recalled. "I don't think playing a highly ranked team to a six- or eight-point loss helps your ball club. I think you have to play to win. I thought, and our players thought, that we could beat LSU."

LSU had an awesomely talented team with two seven-footers, Shaquille O'Neal and Stanley Roberts, and the best college guard in the country, Chris Jackson. Kentucky's trademark had become the three-point shot. The Wildcats had already set several NCAA records for shooting the three. Early in the season sportswriter Billy Reed had named the Wildcats "Pitino's Bambinos," because the players were so young. Late in the year, another sports reporter, John McGill, had changed Bambinos to Bombinos because of their reliance on the three-point shot.

Talking about going into the LSU game, Pitino laughingly recalled, "One of the big strengths we had was when the opposing team stepped on the court, especially a team that had the talent LSU had. When they watched Kentucky warm up, they knew they wouldn't have a problem beating us. Our psychological edge was big because we were so small and scrawny. The other team thought all it had to do was show up to beat us."

Kentucky played its fast-paced style that year with just seven players. Billy Reed dubbed them, "the seven men of iron." Deron Feldhaus and John Pelphrey were the forwards, Reggie Hanson was the starting center and Derrick Miller and Sean Woods operated at the guards. Richie Farmer and Jeff Brassow provided the only relief.

"Not many people thought we could beat LSU but I felt we had a genuine shot to beat them and our team felt that way, too. I knew we would have some defensive problems because of their tremendous size, but I thought, on offense, we could do some things that

Richie Farmer and the Cats kept Chris Jackson off balance most of the game, before the LSU sharpshooter heated up in the second half.

would hurt them. I thought it was imperative that we get the early lead. I was worried that they might go to a zone, but I felt if we could get in front, they would have to play our game. We could spread the floor and make them come out and chase us. I felt that the fact we were small was in our favor. Their big people were going to have to come out on the floor to guard our forwards. Pelphrey and Feldhaus were both good ball handlers and I thought if we could get them to come out on the floor to pick us up, we were quick enough to backdoor them for some easy baskets. I thought the biggest key to our winning the game though, was to make sure we got the lead and make them play our game."

Rick needn't have worried. After the two teams traded three-

Deron Feldhaus and the rest of the Cats had problems maneuvering inside against LSU's 7-1 Shaquille O'Neal.

Sean Woods had some big baskets against LSU in what many observers consider to be one of Rick Pitino's biggest wins at Kentucky.

pointers to start the game, the Wildcats took over. An enthusiastic, if disbelieving, audience watched the Cats roar to a 23-point lead, 41-18. The Bayou Bengals seemed totally confused by UK's pressing defense and began to show some frustration as Roberts batted a ball at one of the officials and was assessed a technical foul.

LSU had too much talent and too much at stake to roll over

and play dead. The Tigers roared back with 14 unanswered points to light up the scoreboard and cut the Wildcat lead to nine, 41-32. The two teams swapped baskets the remainder of the first half and Kentucky led, 48-36.

During the halftime intermission, Pitino cautioned his troops that LSU would make a run. The Tigers' great little guard, Chris Jackson, had connected on only one of his seven three-point attempts in the first half. Rick feared if they let Jackson get on a roll, he could create havoc for the Wildcats in the second half.

Shaquille O'Neal got the second half off to a roaring start for LSU with a thunderous dunk. Kentucky answered with four quick points. That was the way the ebb and flow of the second half played out through much of the game. LSU would make a run...UK would counter. The Tigers closed to within seven, 54-47, then Kentucky pulled away. The Bengals closed later to within eight, 67-59, and once again the Cats pulled away.

Kentucky seemed to be in a comfortable situation with an 87-70 lead with less than six minutes to play since O'Neal had already fouled out. But Pitino's halftime worries were about to happen as Chris Jackson found his eye.

With 2:46 to play, Jackson led the fast break but pulled up and popped a three from 20 feet to cut Kentucky's lead to six, the closest LSU had been since the early minutes of the game.

John Pelphrey and Deron Feldhaus got open on backdoor plays to push the Cats back with a little breathing room. But Jackson was by no means finished. With 1:12 to go, Jackson drove into the right baseline corner and with two Kentucky defenders all over him, his three was right on target. Kentucky 94, LSU 92.

"We were going to run off some clock and try to force LSU to foul us," Pitino recalled. "In that kind of a situation we wanted our best free throw shooters in the game. We had Richie Farmer in there and there's nobody better at the line when it really counts." LSU did foul Farmer, and he went to the line to convert both ends of the one-and-one. Kentucky 96, LSU 92.

Reggie Hanson, one of six Wildcats to score in double figures, slams home two of his 11 points.

Few photos better depict the gigantic feat Kentucky accomplished by knocking off LSU, 100-95.

LSU came down and hurried its shot. It missed. Kentucky got the ball and with Farmer handling the ball most of the time, the Tigers fouled him again. Once again Richie was up to the task and made the one and the bonus. Kentucky 98, LSU 92. Jackson came down and fired from 23 feet, his seventh three-pointer of the game, and with 41 seconds left Kentucky clung to the lead, 98-95.

LSU had to foul quickly and to the Tigers' dismay, the man with the ball again was Farmer. Once more, Richie cashed in both ends of the one and the bonus and that was the old ball game. Kentucky 100, LSU 95.

Rupp Arena went wild. The players were happy but weary. Hanson had played the full 40 minutes. Feldhaus had been on the floor for 39 minutes. LSU's Chris Jackson had a magnificent game with 41 points, but it wasn't enough to offset UK's balance. Six of the seven Kentucky players were in double figures. Derrick Miller had 29, Feldhaus 24, Sean Woods scored 12, Hanson 11 and Pelphrey and Farmer scored 10 apiece. Woods was a big factor in the game. He played less than three minutes in the first half because of foul trouble but scored 10 of his 12 points in the second half. Probably the most telling statistic was turnovers. The Cats made only 13 turnovers for the entire game, while LSU, bothered by UK's swarming press, turned the ball over 27 times. Kentucky outscored LSU 16-4 off turnovers.

The win over LSU pushed Kentucky's record to 13-10 and four of Kentucky's last five games were away from home. The Cats won over Auburn in Rupp by three but lost all four of the road games to finish with the 14-14 record. It was a better record than even the most optimistic person could have hoped for. For his coaching magic, Pitino was named the SEC Coach of the Year and *Basketball News* named him national Coach of the Year. The fans had a ball that season. Pitino not only had given them a better season than any expected, but it was fun to watch the team run and shoot the three-pointers on offense and on defense the Cats played the press from end line to end line.

Pitino had a lot to talk about in his courtside post-game press confer-ence after the Cats pulled off the upset of LSU.

Under the penalties handed down by the NCAA, Kentucky was not permitted to take part in any postseason play, but it was clear that Pitino had brought the Cats farther more quickly than any-one expected. He still looks back on his first Kentucky team with fond memories.

"I think for the fans, the players and for everyone, it was a fun year. I had heard that the Kentucky fans had been coming to the games hoping not to lose instead of hoping to win. I thought they really got into the games that year and it certainly was an enjoyable season for me." Rick thought the win over LSU was the most important game that season. "We beat a team that had three NBA draft picks on it and we went into the game believing we would win it. I think our fans started believing that we were going to definitely build the program back up. What it showed me was that we were on a quicker path of turning around this program than even I anticipated. I thought we could do it if we added one or two big time recruits, added a little size and depth to the program. I thought we could build it back in three years instead of five years. There's no question about it, that win over LSU was the benchmark in our rebuilding program."

What a game! What a season! It might have been only a 14-14 year, but oh my, wasn't it exciting?

Greatest Game Ever?

"Greatest game ever?" Kentucky had just lost a gut-wrenching 104-103 NCAA Tournament game to Duke in overtime. Boston sportswriter Bob Ryan, who was sitting right in front of our broadcasting position, held up a single sheet of notebook paper with the question scrawled on it. It had been a devastating defeat for the Wildcats, but I had to admit it had been a great basketball game.

The Kentucky-Duke game was played on March 28, 1992. To show just how big the game was for Kentucky, we have to turn the calendar back three seasons to 1989.

The NCAA sacked Kentucky with severe penalties, ruling players Eric Manuel and Chris Mills ineligible to play for the Wildcats. Kentucky was forbidden to be on television for a year or to play in a postseason tournament for two years. LeRon Ellis exercised his option to transfer to Syracuse and Sean Sutton went to Lexington Community College for a year before rejoining his dad, Eddie, at Oklahoma State the following season. Eddie, of course, had been the coach at Kentucky during the NCAA investigation. *Sports Illustrated's* cover called it "Kentucky's Shame."

That's the situation Rick Pitino faced when he was brought in to rebuild Kentucky's devastated program. He had only eight scholarship players. None of them was taller than 6-7. Reggie Hanson and Derrick Miller were the only players with starting experience. John Pelphrey, Sean Woods, Deron Feldhaus, Richie Farmer and Jonathan Davis had been bench warmers and Jeff Brassow was the last recruit Eddie Sutton landed before his resignation — not much to get excited about. After I got to know Pitino, I told him if he won 10 games with those players he should be voted Coach of the Year. He did better than that. By firing three-pointers as if they were going out of style, the team finished with a 14-14 record.

Pitino went back to his native New York to bring in a top player for the 1990-91 season and Jamal Mashburn immediately stepped into the starting lineup. The team posted a 22-6 record and actually finished with the best record in the Southeastern Conference but because of the sanctions, could not claim the league championship. The ban on postseason play was still in effect.

The piper had been paid as the 1991-92 season got underway. All the sanctions were gone and the Wildcats could compete on even terms again.

The four seniors were the heart of that 1991-92 Kentucky team. They made up half the squad during Pitino's first season. They were an unlikely lot to be the ones to bring the Wildcats from the ashes, to one of the nation's elite teams, in only three years.

Sean Woods was in Purgatory during the last Eddie Sutton year for academic reasons. John Pelphrey and Deron Feldhaus had been recruited the year before, but so little was thought of their talents that both were redshirted. Richie Farmer came in as a freshman and joined Pelphrey and Feldhaus on the bench during Kentucky's first losing season in 62 years in 1989. Ironically, they started that season by watching Duke paste the Cats by 25 in the Tip-Off Classic.

When Rick Pitino came on board to rebuild the Kentucky program he didn't see much in the way of talent to give him great encouragement. He thought that Reggie Hanson and Derrick Miller were capable of playing at this level, but he doubted the abilities of the other players. Rick had pegged Pelphrey as a smooth-talk-

Sean Woods had an outstanding offensive game in the East Regional final against Duke, as he scored 21 points and had nine assists.

ing locker room lawyer. He felt Woods and Feldhaus couldn't shoot. He looked upon Farmer as an overweight, pampered high school star who would rather hunt and fish than pay the price to be a major college player.

Sutton had been of about the same opinion when he recruited the four. Feldhaus was the first to sign. He came aboard early. He was the son of a former Wildcat, Allen Sr., and had played for his father at Mason County. Sutton perceived Deron as a player who could come off the bench and offer some relief.

Pelphrey came out of high school the same year as Feldhaus and it was Pelphrey who earned the honor of "Mr. Basketball" that year. He was quite a star for Paintsville, but Sutton's staff did not feel he could play at UK. C.M. Newton was vigorously recruiting him at Vanderbilt, but it was not until Louisville got interested did Kentucky offer him a scholarship. John grabbed it immediately.

The next season Farmer came out of Clay County, one of the greatest players the mountains had ever produced. He had been All-State for three straight years. He had led his team to the state high school championship. His senior year, he was named "Mr. Basketball." Yet Kentucky didn't come calling. The UK coaching staff thought he did not know how to move without the ball and could not play defense. Richie was such a legend in Eastern Kentucky, the fans insisted he become a Wildcat. Sutton relented and offered him a scholarship.

When Pitino first got to Kentucky he was appalled at the team's lack of physical conditioning. He brought in Ray "Rock" Oliver to whip the players into shape. Oliver brought a drill sergeant's mentality into the program and he drove the players hard. Rock did it with an even hand and, actually, was very popular with the players.

By the time Pelphrey, Feldhaus, Farmer and Woods had reached their senior year, they had been joined by a sophomore who was to become a great Kentucky player. Jamal Mashburn brought star-quality to the lineup. Freshman Gimel Martinez had also worked his way into the starting lineup. And Dale Brown transferred from a junior college and certainly made a tremendous contribution to the team.

Mashburn, without question, brought another dimension to the team for the 1991-92 season and Martinez brought some extra height. But the four seniors were the heart and soul of that team.

With Martinez starting at center and Mashburn at forward, three of the seniors were in the lineup. Woods was the point guard and, over three seasons, Pitino had convinced Sean that the job of a point guard was to make everyone else on the team better.

Farmer started at the two guard. He had lost 20 pounds since his sophomore season but still had the guts of a burglar. Richie was tremendous in the clutch and welcomed the chance to take the last shot to decide a game.

Pelphrey started at the forward position opposite Mashburn. John was the real leader on that ball club. Extremely well liked by all the other players, "Pel" often called team meetings and on the court he was extremely intelligent and an outstanding passer.

Feldhaus was the sixth man on that team and he filled the role admirably. A totally unselfish player, Deron almost always gave the team a lift when he entered the game.

For the 1991-92 season, all sanctions were gone. For the first time in three years the Cats could look forward to postseason play.

It was such a nice and unassuming group that Pitino wondered if it was made up of the right stuff for much of a run. "We're just a bunch of wallflowers," he told me. "I'm afraid while everybody else is dancing; our players will be standing in the back of the room."

Kentucky opened the season in the NIT Preseason Tournament. The Wildcats waltzed past West Virginia in Rupp Arena, but were shocked in the next game on their home court by Pittsburgh, 85-67. Kentucky lost other games that season, but I thought it was the only time the Cats went into a game fat-headed and extremely overconfident.

The early exit from the NIT gave Pitino almost two weeks before the next game and he worked the players hard. The most important thing he did was convince the players that they would have to leave it all on the floor every game to be any good.

That team lost a few but never again did it fail to go down fighting. Still, UK won 23 and lost only six during the regular season which was a better record than I thought the team would attain.

The Kentucky players were very excited about heading for Birmingham and their first postseason tournament in two years. I flew down with them on their chartered plane, and several UK fans met us at the Birmingham Airport. There was still another group that met the team when it arrived at the hotel. Everybody was excited the Cats were about to embark on postseason play in the SEC Tournament.

First up was Vanderbilt. His freshman season, Mashburn had felt that the team belonged to Reggie Hanson. This season he felt it was the seniors' team. He was a completely unselfish player, and midway through the first half, Pitino had to take him out for a good butt-chewing for not shooting. He threatened to keep him out for the rest of the game. The threat was short-lived and when Mash went back in, he went to war. He ended up with 24 points and 10 rebounds as Kentucky claimed a 76-57 win. Mash stayed at war for the rest of the postseason.

LSU was next for Kentucky in one of the semifinals. The Tigers had won convincingly during the regular season, but this time LSU had to go without its best player, Shaquille O'Neal. He had been involved in a fight against Tennessee and was suspended for the Kentucky game. Pitino warned his players about the "wounded tiger," feeling the other players would fight even harder without their superstar. LSU gave a great effort and Kentucky had to play hard to come away with an 80-74 victory.

Kentucky would play Alabama in the SEC Tournament championship game. The Cats hadn't won an official title since 1986. Their 1988 title had been vacated in the aftermath of the NCAA sanctions. Alabama came into the Kentucky game off a very rugged win over Arkansas and was favored to measure UK in the final. It was a tough first half, with Alabama holding a 32-29 lead as Hollywood Robinson hit a three-pointer just ahead of the buzzer.

As the team left the dressing room for the second half, Mashburn, never one to be very vocal, called the team together and said, "We've got to start playing harder."

In what I thought was the team's best offensive half of the season up to that point, Kentucky overwhelmed Alabama over the next 20 minutes and won going away, 80-54. Mashburn was named the MVP and Pelphrey joined him on the All-Tournament Team.

While still in Birmingham, the players learned they would be the No. 2 seed in the East and would open their NCAA play against Old Dominion in Worcester, Massachusetts. For the four seniors, their first NCAA Tournament appearance was a reality.

I always taped Rick's pre-game program during the team's walk-through on game day. I had never seen him as nervous as he was the day of the game with Old Dominion. Perhaps the team sensed his uneasiness and had to just go out there and gut out an 88-69 win. On his post-game radio program, Rick admitted it was the most nervous he had ever been as a coach. I suppose, after the team had come so far, he didn't want to see them ambushed right out of the starting gate.

The win over Old Dominion moved UK to a second-round game against Iowa State. This time both teams shot the lights out, and with all four of the seniors scoring in double figures, Kentucky finally pulled out a 106-98 decision. The Wildcats had advanced to the Sweet 16 and the way I looked at it, anything from there on out was gravy.

The next week Kentucky moved on to the East Regional to play Massachusetts in Philadelphia's Spectrum. With Mashburn scoring 30 points, Kentucky came away with an 87-77 win to move into the final against Duke. The winner would advance to the Final Four, but most felt it would be a walk-over for the Blue Devils.

Duke was the defending national champion. The Blue Devils

Jamal Mashburn came up big, although his 28 points against Duke in the regional championship weren't quite enough.

came into the game against Kentucky ranked No. 1 in the nation. Only Pitino and his players felt they had a chance. Rick noted that Duke was bigger and more talented. He felt the only advantage his team had was that no one was in better physical shape than the Wildcats. He also felt that he needed to put in a new defense for the Duke game. Kentucky had full-court pressed its way to the Elite Eight, but Pitino was fearful against a team with Duke's size and speed, all of his players would foul out.

He decided to pick up full-court, but once the ball passed the center stripe, the Cats would drop back into a 2-3 zone. Pitino liked the way his players were approaching the game. The day before, at a press conference, Richie Farmer had said of Duke, "We respect 'em, but we don't fear 'em."

Nobody, of course, expected one of the greatest college games ever played, but that's exactly what happened. Pelphrey got the scoring started with a three-pointer. After Woods connected from the field, treys by Pel and Mashburn, put the Cats in front 11-6. Kentucky's lead grew to eight after Martinez hit a three, 20-12. That was the biggest lead of the game for the Cats and by halftime Duke was in front by five, 50-45.

With Pelphrey having committed three fouls, Pitino started Feldhaus in the second half. Duke began to slowly inch away from the Cats until the Blue Devils led by 12, 67-55. Martinez had already fouled out and with 11:08 to go, Pitino called a timeout.

Rick told his players they were going to abandon the zone and now unleash their man-to-man press the full 94 feet of the court. He said, "The press is going to take its toll. We're going to win this game." What followed was the best basketball game I ever saw.

The level of play by both teams had been high but both teams now turned it up a notch. After the timeout, Kentucky ran off the next eight points on a close-in shot by Dale Brown and two three-pointers by Mashburn. Let the game begin!

Duke, with its great talent and tradition, fought back, but the team's frustration was most evident when Christian Laettner put his foot in the stomach of UK freshman Aminu Timberlake, who was lying helpless on the floor. The officials tagged Laettner with a technical foul.

There was less than six minutes left to play when Kentucky finally caught the Blue Devils at 81-81, on Woods' three-point shot.

Although this wasn't "the" shot, Christian Laettner had plenty of key baskets that helped Duke survive a furious Cat rally.

Two free throws by Grant Hill pushed Duke back on top, 83-81. Mashburn answered to tie it at 83-all with a drive to the basket.

Duke pushed the lead out to three points but Feldhaus broke for the basket and Pelphrey hit him with a perfect pass to cut the Duke lead to one. Dale Brown's three-pointer pushed Kentucky to a two-point lead, 89-87. Duke, scoring on a jump shot by Brian Davis tied it yet again. Woods hit a pair of free throws for Kentucky and Laettner added a pair from the charity line for Duke. After a UK turnover, Thomas Hill's jumper pushed Duke ahead 93-91. Kentucky was up to the challenge. Pelphrey missed with a jump shot but Feldhaus got the rebound and twisted like a pretzel as he got it back up and in to knot the count at 93-all. Bobby Hurley missed an off-balance jumper and it was going to overtime. Lordy, how much could the old ticker take?

The game lost none of its intensity as the extra five minutes began. As he had done at the outset of the game, Pelphrey connected for a three to get the Cats away to the lead.

Pitino had warned his players to guard against Duke's three-pointers, but Hurley let one fly and missed. Grant Hill took the long rebound and pitched it back out to Hurley. This time the guard was right on target to tie at 96-96. Pelphrey fired in a basket for Kentucky and Laettner canned a pair of free throws for Duke and it was even, 98-98. Woods made a beautiful move to the basket, but missed the shot and Duke got the rebound. Duke coach Mike Krzyzewski called a timeout. Only 54 seconds remained.

With less than a minute to play, the score tied, every possession, every play would be crucial. Pitino told his forces that Duke would go to Laettner. He wanted his players to double down on him but not to foul.

Duke worked the ball to their star and with a crowd of blue-shirted Kentuckians grabbing at the ball, Laettner rose for a jump shot that kissed off the glass and into the net. It was the most difficult shot he had made the entire game, and it put Duke up by two, 100-98.

Kentucky came down court and worked the ball around the perimeter until Mashburn spotted an opening along the baseline and he went for it. Mash put up a short bank shot that was good. Antonio Lang was beaten on the play and fouled Mashburn. After Mash converted the free throw, Kentucky led again, 101-100. Kentucky called a timeout with 19.7 seconds left.

Pitino told the players that they would not call a timeout if Duke scored. Kentucky was operating well against the Blue Devils' defense and he did not want Duke to have a chance to change defenses during a timeout. He again told his players to double down on Laettner who would very likely take the shot.

Duke did work the ball to Laettner and Mashburn dropped back to double the Duke All-American. Unfortunately, in trying to strip the ball, Mash committed his fifth foul, and with 14 seconds left, Laettner went to the line for two shots. He made both to push Duke back on top, 102-101. Pitino inserted Farmer for Mashburn. All four seniors were now on the floor.

As Kentucky brought the ball down court, Pitino changed his mind and called a timeout with 7.8 seconds left. This time he told Woods to penetrate the middle and if Duke picked him up, dish the ball out to the wing. Rick felt Kentucky could not stop Duke from scoring with any time left on the clock. He wanted to take the last shot. "I wanted to win or lose the game on the last possession," he said.

Farmer passed the ball inbounds to Woods, who gave Hurley a head fake and ran past him to the key. Heading down the lane, Woods saw Laettner switch over to help out defensively, but he was too far into his move to stop now. He rose for his jump shot as the 6-11 Laettner tried to block it. Somehow Sean got it away and it hit above the rim and banked in. Kentucky had the lead 103-102.

The Duke players all seemed to be calling timeout. The clock showed 2.1 seconds remaining.

There was no secret what Duke would do. With so little time remaining and with the Blue Devils having to cover the length of the court, there would be a long pass. Almost surely, it would go to Laettner.

The problem was Kentucky's. Pitino pondered whether to put a defensive man on the Duke player who would make the inbounds pass, or double team Laettner. Laettner was four inches taller than

Sean Woods hit what seemed to be the game-winning basket that gave Kentucky a 103-102 lead with 2.1 seconds left.

Kentucky's tallest player on the court. Martinez and Mashburn were on the bench with five fouls. Pelphrey and Feldhaus, both at 6-7, were the only players he had with any height. Pitino decided to put the two men on Laettner.

For Duke, the pass had to be absolutely perfect. Laettner had to make the shot.

Grant Hill, a superb athlete, took the ball out of bounds. Laettner lined up on the side of the floor. As Hill uncorked the long pass that traveled 75 feet, Laettner broke into the top of the key. Pelphrey went for the ball but the bigger man came down with it. Feldhaus was behind Laettner. The Duke star faked right, put down a dribble and turned to his right for the jump shot. It was perfect. Duke had won 104-103 in overtime.

The Kentucky players were devastated. Duke's coach, Mike Krzyzewski, was a gracious and classy man. He saw the devastation on Farmer's face. "Just looking at his face, there was no way I could be celebrating," he said. Krzyzewski went to Farmer. "I'm sorry Richie," he said. "I'm so sorry."

Back in the UK dressing room, Rick tried to tell the players how proud he was of them. He brought out the old *Sports Illustrated* cover that shouted, "Kentucky's Shame." He told them how they had brought the Kentucky program back. He tried everything he could think of to try and lift their spirits. "The harder I tried, the more they wept," he said.

At courtside, I was signing off on my final UK broadcast after a 39-year run. I looked up and Coach K signaled he would like to say something to the UK listeners. "They were absolutely sensational," he said of the Kentucky players. "I feel bad for them. I hope you believe that."

"Greatest game ever?" That's what Bob Ryan of the *Boston Globe* had scribbled on a sheet of paper and held up to me. I was in too much shock to give Bob much of an answer that night, but I'll answer him now. It was the greatest game I ever saw. The "wallflowers" had danced a beautiful dance.

A Season of Thrills

The 1993-94 Kentucky team had more than its share of thrills. Certainly, the 31-point comeback against LSU was the highlight of the season. That history-making game was so remarkable that it will be the trademark of that team and that miraculous Wildcat victory deserves its own chapter. While it would be impossible to top that game, there were other exciting moments to that Kentucky season.

Personally, the most memorable part of the season was the trip to Hawaii. During the summer of 1993, Rick Pitino had invited Frances and me to go along with the team as his guests. The following December, we were winging our way westward to Hawaii for the Maui Classic.

I had been away from the broadcasts for almost two years and I don't think I realized just how much I missed being around Pitino and the team. My colleagues sometimes think I'm odd, but I enjoy watching practice almost as much as watching the game. I really get a kick out of looking on as a coach puts in the game plan, then watching during the game to see how that plan works out. I went to every practice the team had in Maui. I remember that first one. The team had its own bus for the tournament and its own special driver. This man named Joe was very familiar with the Kentucky program. Even though he was a native of Maui, Joe had gone to college at Eastern Kentucky University, in Richmond, and he had even tried out for Roy Kidd's football team. Joe drove the team to this small high school gym that was located up on a hill overlooking Lahaina, the town where the tournament was held. While the team was warming up during drills before practice, Rodrick Rhodes went in for a thunderous dunk and that glass backboard shattered all over the floor in a zillion pieces. The players didn't know whether to laugh or get set for some sharp words from Pitino. The Kentucky coach ignored the whole thing. Since the gym had only two baskets, Pitino simply moved the team to the other end of the court and practice went on as usual.

The Wildcats' first game in the Maui Classic was against the Texas Longhorns. The game was close early, but Kentucky pulled away to win easily, 86-61.

Ohio State was next on the agenda, and with Travis Ford and Tony Delk combining for 50 points, the Cats waltzed, 100-88.

Rick invited Frances and me to join the team for dinner after the game. We sat with Rick and his wife Joanne, Father Bradley and Bill Keightley. The Cats were to face an outstanding Arizona team for the championship and Rick was especially concerned with the guard tandem of Khalid Reeves and Damon Stoudamire. Pitino felt the two were the best pair of starting guards in all of college basketball. "They both can kill you with the three," he said, "and they both can take you one-on-one and beat you."

Kentucky fans follow the team anywhere it goes and without question, the UK fans far outnumbered those from any of the other teams in the tournament. It was mostly a blue-clad crowd that packed into the Lahaina Civic Center as Kentucky faced Lute Olson's undefeated Arizona team. Two teams that liked to run and gun began a race-horse type of game that turned into a classic.

Kentucky was quicker out of the starting gate and the Cats raced to an early 19-12 lead. With Stoudamire having a sensational first half, including four baskets from three-point range, the

Travis Ford earned most valuable player honors at the Maui Classic and SEC Tournament to highlight a memorable senior campaign.

The Kentucky bench savors a soon-to-be title as the clock winds down in the championship game of the SEC Tournament.

Wildcats were unable to put it away. Still, Kentucky was ahead by eight at the intermission, 49-41.

The Cats tightened their defense on Stoudamire during the

second half and he was able to fire only one three-point shot that was wide of the mark. But Reeves got on track and kept Arizona right in the hunt. It was his three-pointer with 6:25 left in the game that gave Arizona its first lead. From there until the final buzzer it was a dogfight.

With only 1:25 to play, and Kentucky clinging to a 91-90 lead, Tony Delk was suffering severe leg cramps in the hot-box of a gym and Kentucky called a timeout. Jeff Brassow was sent into the game for the ailing Delk.

The Cats put the ball in play and, as the shot clock wound down, Rhodes took a shot that was off-target but Brassow came down with the rebound. The officials went over to the sideline and watched a video tape replay and came to the conclusion that Rhodes' shot had not touched the rim and that the shot clock had run out on the Wildcats. Arizona was awarded the ball out of bounds. Reeves worked the ball downcourt, and as he drove off the left side of the key, Rhodes reached in and was called for the foul. Reeves converted on both free throws and Arizona moved into the lead, 92-91. Only 5.5 seconds remained in the game.

Kentucky had to move the ball the length of the court and get off the shot. It would have to come quickly. Rhodes and Brassow broke to the wings. The ball came to Rhodes and he went streaking down the right side of the court. As the clock was about to run out, Rod let a long three-pointer fly. It was no good, but Brassow came racing in, and with one-tenth of a second left, he tipped it in to give Kentucky a heart-stopping, 93-92 victory.

"There wasn't time to try to run a play," Brassow was saying recently. "When Rod got the ball he was running down the right side. I knew he had to take the last shot so I ran for the basket down the left side of the floor. The shot came off to the left side and I just happened to be in the perfect spot. I knew there wasn't enough time to do anything but tip it. Fortunately, it went in just as the horn sounded."

All hell broke loose. Kentucky fans were charging from the

stands toward the playing floor. The players were jumping up and down and hugging each other and the usually cool Pitino came charging on the court like a bull. "I thought he was going to tackle me," Brassow laughed.

Ford had a terrific tournament and was named the Maui MVP, but that one game belonged to Brassow. "It was the most exciting game for me personally in my career at Kentucky," Brassow said. "There were maybe better team efforts like the comeback against LSU or making it to the Final Four, but, personally, that was my biggest thrill. I'll never forget it as long as I live."

The 1993-94 season was a bizarre one. It had more than its share of strange events — of highs and lows. One of the low points came in the SEC opener in Rupp Arena against Vanderbilt. It changed the Kentucky team for the rest of the season. The Cats won handily, 107-82, but, in the first half, the starting UK center, Rodney Dent, went down with an injury that was to end his college career. Dent, the man his teammates called "Moon" was Kentucky's only big, strong inside player at 6-11, 240 pounds. He was the most consistent scorer inside and he had the muscle to force the opponents' big people out of the post with his defense. To Pitino's credit, he was upbeat about the Cats' future without Dent, but almost every good center feasted on UK the rest of the campaign.

Dent's misfortune took away some of the glitter from a remarkable record Ford set in that game. Travis went eight-for-eight from the free throw line to give him 46 consecutive free throws. This broke the old UK record of 40, which had been held by Jim Master. The next game against Notre Dame, Travis broke the SEC record of 47 which was held by Vanderbilt's Phil Cox, a Kentuckian from Harlan County. Trav's 50 consecutive free throws is the conference record. Ironically, it was at the free throw line that Ford enjoyed his most shining moment of the season and it was also at the free throw line he suffered his greatest embarrassment.

There's an old cliché that goes "what goes around, comes around." In the 1970s, Kentucky and Tennessee were locked in a tough game in Memorial Coliseum. One of the key plays happened when the Vols' outstanding player, Ernie Grunfeld, shot two free throws, making both, that should have been taken by a teammate with less talent at the charity stripe. Just how much bearing Grunfeld's antics had on the outcome of the game is debatable, but Tennessee won.

Kentucky players used the same bad judgement in the return game with Vanderbilt in 1994, this time in Nashville, not once but twice. Gimel Martinez volunteered to shoot free throws for Jared Prickett and Ford suggested to Walter McCarty that he take the shots that should have gone to Andre Riddick. Kentucky won the game 77-69. Travis compounded the problem when he made a joke of it in a post-game interview with a reporter.

When Pitino learned of the indiscretion, he was livid. I was really proud of the UK coach who insisted that integrity was more important than victory. He suspended Ford, Martinez and Prickett for the next game, which was a very important SEC battle against Tennessee in Knoxville.

With only eight players, the Wildcats fought and clawed their way to a 77-73 decision. It was one of the most courageous efforts ever by a Kentucky team.

I still go to most of the Kentucky home games and from time to time I like to go by the dressing room after the game. It was during that season that Pitino said to me, on one occasion, that it was the hardest team to coach that he had ever had. He didn't elaborate, but I felt it was a team that never really did totally come together. Anybody in his right mind would know Mashburn would be missed, but I think his departure hurt the other players as well as just losing his magnificent talent. I thought his absence especially hurt Ford and Prickett. With Mash down in the paint, opponents couldn't concentrate on stopping Travis out on the perimeter. Arkansas coach Nolan Richardson made no bones about it. He said that Ford was the head of that Kentucky team and "if you cut off the head, the body will die." Travis was a marked man without

Pitino had a great asset in Travis Ford, who served as a very capable floor general throughout his career.

Mashburn to take off the pressure. I thought too, that without Mash, Prickett was a marked man down inside and he didn't have the kind of year he had the previous season as a freshman. With Mashburn turning pro after his junior campaign and Dent's loss midway through the 1993-94 season, it was too much to overcome.

Even though that was an excellent UK team, it lacked that special ingredient to win a national championship.

The Cats went to South Carolina to close out the regular season. The Gamecocks had won only three league games, and all the Wildcats had to do was win to gain the SEC's East Division Championship and the accompanying No. 1 seed in the league tournament. With a lethargic Wildcat performance, South Carolina upset Kentucky 75-74. So much for Kentucky's tournament chances. Oh ye of little faith.

Pitino has been a master at getting his teams ready for SEC Tournament games and this was to be no exception. With Tony Delk pulling the trigger for 29 points, the Cats rolled over Mississippi State 95-76, to set up a rematch with the nation's top-ranked team, Arkansas.

The tournament was being played in The Pyramid in Memphis and Kentucky found itself in an unusual situation. With Arkansas located just across the river, the Razorback fans outnumbered those in blue. The Hogs had beaten Kentucky 90-82 in Rupp Arena during the regular season and came into the SEC Tournament ranked No. 1 in the nation.

The Cats set a tournament record with 16 three-pointers and proved too much for Arkansas, 90-78, to move into the final against Florida.

The two teams had split their games during the season with Florida winning at home by two and Kentucky gaining a three-point win in Rupp Arena. In Memphis it was all Kentucky as the Cats prevailed, 73-60. Ford, Brassow and Delk made the All-Tournament Team with Travis being named MVP. It was Pitino's third SEC Tournament title in a row. Arkansas and Florida would go on

The 73-60 win in the championship game of the SEC Tournament made it three in a row for the Wildcats under Rick Pitino.

to the NCAA Tournament with both advancing to the Final Four and Arkansas winning the championship.

Kentucky began play in the NCAA Tournament in St. Petersburg, Florida. The Cats showed opening-game jitters in the first half against Tennessee State, but caught fire in the final twenty

minutes and pulled away to an easy 83-70 victory.

Andre Riddick had his best game as a Wildcat, scoring 22 points and dominating TSU's outstanding center, Carlos Rogers.

Kentucky was the higher seed and favored to measure Marquette in the second round of the NCAA Tournament. The Warriors had a huge front line, and Kentucky always had trouble after Dent's injury when an opponent had big, talented inside players. Marquette proved the point again as Kentucky shot miserably

The 1994 SEC Tournament title, the third during his UK career, was especially gratifying for Jeff Brassow, who overcame injuries again and again to comeback and contribute at guard.

from the perimeter and the Warriors sent Kentucky home early. Marquette won the game, 75-63.

After going to the Final Four the previous season, Kentucky fans were disappointed with the Cats' quick exit from the NCAA. Still, looking back, the 1993-94 season was a very good year. UK won 27 and lost seven, a record any team would point to with pride. That team won the SEC Tournament for the third straight year. And, oh my, what thrills it gave us along the way: the tip-in to win the Maui Classic, the phenomenal 31-point comeback to beat LSU, Travis Ford setting the consecutive free throw record, and the big free throw "switcheroo" at Vanderbilt.

Four seniors who brought a great deal to the UK program departed after that season. "Moon" Dent left prematurely following his injury and his loss was felt the remainder of the campaign. Ford, Martinez and Brassow completed their eligibility — Ford, after transferring from Missouri and undergoing knee surgery, came back for two marvelous seasons with Kentucky. He was one of the premier point guards in the game and as a junior was very instrumental in helping the Cats get to the Final Four. Gimel Martinez lacked the bulk Kentucky needed inside, but he had great hands and was a good shooter from inside, outside and from the free throw line. What can I say about Jeff Brassow? He was forced to undergo knee surgery three times. Each time he came back to play. Sure, he played with pain but he also played with courage. Jeff was at his best when the chips were down.

That 1993-94 season was one of my favorites. Those players certainly gave us enough thrills for a dozen campaigns.

The Miracle of Fat Tuesday

The date was February 15, 1994. It was Fat Tuesday, the last day of carnival before the beginning of Lent, normally a day for celebration in Baton Rouge, Louisiana.

It was a situation that Richard Allen Pitino had experienced many times in his almost 17 years as a basketball coach. His team was trailing at halftime. Kentucky had trailed by as many as 21 points in the first half but had cut the margin to 16 by intermission and Pitino was actually feeling good about the Wildcats' chances as he trailed them into the dressing room in the Pete Maravich Assembly Center on the Louisiana State University campus. He felt LSU was shooting too quickly and had been fortunate in making some bad shots. "I thought at that point, there was no problem to our winning the game," he said.

Just before sending the team back out for the second half, Pitino gave the players the age-old admonition to take their time, not to try to catch up all at once but to show some patience.

If Pitino's belief that those bad LSU shots would stop falling, it certainly wasn't apparent as the second half got underway. The Bayou Bengals were on fire, and they almost doubled their halftime lead, stretching it to 31 points.

Pitino felt LSU had been in what he called a "zone" in the first half and that the Tigers would tail off as the game went along. With LSU leading, 50-37, the sky fell in on the Wildcats as the Tigers ran off 18 straight points.

After LSU extended the lead to 20 points at 57-37, Pitino called timeout to try and stop the bleeding. He did his best to look confident, feeling that if the coach lacked confidence, the team certainly would.

LSU continued to connect for three-pointers and, shortly after the timeout, Travis Ford was so frustrated he committed an intentional foul. That resulted in two points from the free throw line. On the ensuing inbounds play, Jamie Brandon arched in a three-pointer. At 62-37, a 25-point lead now for LSU, Pitino called another timeout. "I just tried to keep a superior attitude," Pitino said.

Rick Pitino took many a long look skyward during the first 25 minutes of the game in Baton Rouge.

"I wanted them to know I still believed in them."

LSU struck for three more field goals to complete an 18-0 run and push the score to 68-37, a 31-point lead. No team in basketball history had overcome such a lead on the road and it looked like an LSU blowout. "I remember sitting there on the bench right at that time," Jeff Brassow recalled. Ford had left the game after the intentional foul and Brassow turned to his teammate and said, "I can't believe this is happening. This shouldn't be happening to us." Only 15 minutes and 34 seconds remained to be played. The stage was set for one of the greatest comebacks in sports history.

Rodrick Rhodes was fouled driving to the basket and converted both free throws. Chris Harrison banked his jump shot off the board and the next time downcourt, after Ford missed from the outside, Andre Riddick put in the rebound and Kentucky had cut the LSU lead to 26 points, 68-43. Tiger coach Dale Brown, called a timeout.

At the UK bench, Pitino told his team, "Look, we've cut a little off. Let's cut a little more off and make 'em call another timeout."

It was only 1:47 later that LSU did call another timeout but this time it was not signaled by Coach Brown. Kentucky had really picked up its defense, and when Andre Owens was caught in a two-man-trap near midcourt, he called for the timeout to keep from losing the ball. The score was LSU 70, Kentucky 48. The Tigers led by 22 with 12:22 left to play.

Pitino continued to implore his troops to chip away at the LSU lead a little at a time. "I told them," he said, "to try to get it within 15 points and that we would get one of our runs going."

The Kentucky run was about to start. Rhodes drove in for a basket. Harrison, back in the game, was well outside the key and the LSU defense, perhaps not knowing that Harrison's forté was shooting, backed off him. Chris arched in a perfect rainbow from behind the three-point arc to cut the Tiger lead to 17, 70-53 with 11:27 to play. "We had really been missing the three-pointers," Brassow pointed out, "and when Chris hit one, I think that really changed the momentum of the game. We seemed to seize the tempo from LSU."

After Brandon cashed in a pair of free throws, McCarty fired in a three. Gimel Martinez tried his hand from three-point range but missed. Tony Delk grabbed the rebound on the right side of the basket, then slipped a short pass to McCarty on the other side for an easy layup. Apparently LSU had little in its scouting report on Harrison, because once again the Tiger defense backed off and Chris fired in another three-pointer. UK had outscored the Tigers 18-2 over a span of a little more than four minutes and had cut 20 points off the seemingly insurmountable 31-point LSU lead. The Tigers still held the advantage, 72-61, with 9:52 left in the game.

After LSU pushed the lead back up to 16, it was time for Brassow to do his number.

Jeff Brassow was a fifth-year senior on that team that was destined to participate in one of sports' greatest comebacks. He had been the last player recruited by Eddie Sutton and was the only player on the squad that Pitino had not brought to Kentucky. Brassow was looking forward to the game against LSU. "I've always loved that gym," Jeff related. "Even though the team hasn't fared very well at LSU through the years, I've always been able to score well there. It's a good place for me to play. I've had some of my better games down there."

After Ronnie Henderson had hit one of his eight baskets from behind the three-point line, LSU moved ahead, 77-61. On the next trip downcourt, Brassow found himself left alone by the LSU defense and he broke for the basket and kissed it in off the glass to cut the advantage to 77-63. After another LSU field goal, Brassow found himself wide open in the left corner and he fired in a perfect three to cut the lead to 13 as LSU held a dwindling 79-66 lead. After an LSU miss, McCarty rebounded the ball and passed it out to Travis Ford. He slipped a short pass to Brassow and after one dribble, Jeff fired in another three from outside. The margin now was down to 10, 79-69.

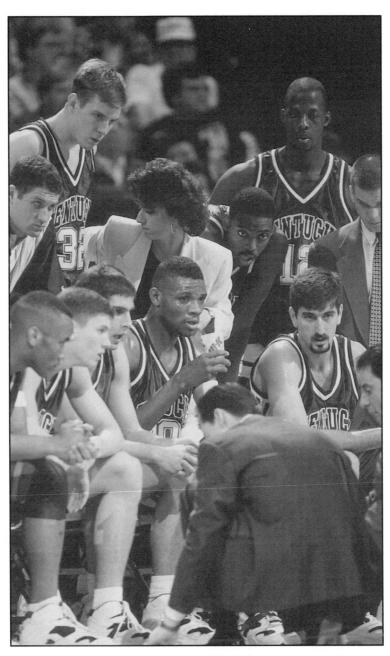

After many sideline conversations, the Kentucky players responded and the improbable became reality.

LSU pushed the lead back to 13 with three points from the free throw line. Rodrick Rhodes checked back in, committed two quick fouls, but then hit his only three-pointer of the game. Taking a pass from Ford in the backcourt, Rhodes moved behind a perfect screen set by Martinez and cut the LSU lead back to 10, 82-72.

The Tigers were never to lead by more than 10 points again, even though they did lead by 10 on two later occasions. The last lead by that margin came with 3:57 to play, 88-78.

Martinez was fouled after rebounding a missed LSU free throw. He made the first but missed the second. Delk came up with the rebound and the Cats worked the perimeter until Ford got open for a three out of the deep left corner. LSU's lead was reduced to six, 88-82, with 3:41 to play.

LSU built the lead to nine and was leading by seven when Brassow got in on the action again. Brandon was bringing the ball upcourt for the Tigers when Brassow slapped the ball away. Riddick came up with the ball and fed it upcourt to Harrison. Chris found Brassow open on the left side and Jeff fired in still another three-pointer to cut the lead to four, 91-87.

Clarence Ceasar cashed in two free throws to move LSU back to a 93-87 lead and it was time for Brassow to continue his act.

"I was feeling really good about my shot by that time," he said, "and we needed to be putting up good shots. Travis and I had a little screen and roll play up at the top and I was going to try to get Travis open for the three. The LSU players got caught a little bit in their switch and Travis switched the ball to me and I just stepped back behind the NBA line and let it go." Brassow's extremely long three-point try was right on target and Kentucky was within three, 93-90.

LSU was struggling at the free throw line. Everybody that is, except Ceasar. He fired in two more to make it 95-90. Tony Delk got a double screen on the left side and found himself wide open for a three. Good! Kentucky was within two, 95-93.

Both teams went cold. Both teams made turnovers. Brassow

A spirited post-game celebration was in order after the Cats finished their unprecedented rally from 31 points down to beat LSU, 99-95.

went to the free throw line but missed both tosses. After a couple of tips at the basket, the ball went out of bounds but was touched last by LSU. Only 51 seconds remained.

Ford drove into the middle but lost the ball and once again LSU touched it before it went out of bounds. Brassow put the ball in play from under the Kentucky basket. The Cats worked it around the perimeter. Delk drove down the middle and pitched it out to McCarty in the left corner. He was right in front of the UK

With 19 seconds left, Walter McCarty capped the comeback when he hit the biggest three-pointer of his career to give Kentucky a 96-95 lead.

bench and Pitino yelled to McCarty "Take it, Walt. And count it." McCarty drilled a three and Kentucky took the lead for the first time since Andre Riddick's free throw in the first minute of the game made it 1-0 Wildcats. Now they led 96-95, but there were still 19 seconds to play.

LSU brought the ball over midcourt and called a timeout with 11.5 seconds to play.

Gathered around the UK bench, Brassow remembered, "Coach Pitino was looking me dead in the eye and I could tell he was thinking if he should take me out for defensive purposes. As it turned out, it was my man who tried to take me one-on-one." Brandon drove with Brassow guarding him every step of the way. The shot was no good and Delk was fouled after taking the rebound. With just over four seconds left, Tony hit one of two to give the Cats a 97-95 lead.

Pitino put Jared Prickett on Ceasar, who took the ball out of bounds. Ceasar threw a long pass to Sean Gipson at the LSU free throw line and when Martinez challenged the pass, Gipson fell down with the ball and was called for steps. That, for all intents and purposes, was the old ball game. Ford hit two free throws to end the game and Kentucky had finished one of the most miraculous comebacks in sports history with a 99-95 win over LSU.

"We were just screaming and yelling when we got back to the dressing room," Brassow said. "It was a big win for us. We had come back from 31 points down and we had lost two in a row going into that game. We were giving each other high fives. We just could not believe what we had done. It's something I know I'll always remember." So will all Kentucky fans.

That night, I did something I had never done before. The game had been telecast on ESPN, and the network was going to replay the game at 3:30 a.m. I set my alarm for 4 a.m. and got up and savored that second half all over again. It wasn't nearly as nerve-racking the second time, knowing the outcome ahead of time.

Back From the Dead, Twice

Rodrick Rhodes broke my heart. Not because he went to the free throw line for two shots with one second to play and the score tied and he missed them both, but what caring soul could fail to feel great compassion for a young man thrust into such a pressure-packed situation. That sticks out especially in my memory of one of the greatest games ever played.

Kentucky fans, as they always do, looked ahead to a great season as the Wildcats suited up for the 1994-95 season. True, four seasoned veterans had departed, but four starters would be returning. Travis Ford would be missed as the starting point guard and so would valuable reserves Jeff Brassow, Gimel Martinez and Rodney Dent, who missed the last half of the season with an injury. Joining eight lettermen, Rick Pitino would welcome Mark Pope, who sat out a season after transferring from the University of Washington, plus freshmen Antoine Walker, Allen Edwards and Scott Padgett. Walker, in particular, was bringing in very impressive credentials as one of the best freshmen in the country and Pitino was even comparing him to All-American Jamal Mashburn when Mashburn was a freshman.

If there's a bigger or better rivalry in college basketball than the Kentucky-Arkansas series, it has escaped detection. The two Southeastern Conference powers met in Fayetteville on January 29, 1995, and if anybody was disappointed in the caliber of play in that one, it hasn't been recorded. Scotty Thurman's three-point basket with 11 seconds left in the game gave Arkansas a thrilling 94-92 win over the Cats in a game many observers thought was the best game of the season played anywhere in the country. It was filled with intensity. It saw first one team make a run, then the other, and the emotion was sky-high from start to finish. Tony Delk was magnificent in defeat, scoring a career-high 31 points. Arkansas won the day but Kentucky won the regular season SEC championship. The two teams would meet again in the conference tournament and that game, if anything, was even better than the first.

To set up the rematch, Kentucky had to beat Auburn and Florida in the SEC Tournament. The Cats won both and looked very impressive in dispatching the Tigers and the Gators to move into the title game against Arkansas.

Even though people were still talking about the great game the two teams had played during the regular season, Pitino said it was not really a great game. "It was a high-scoring, entertaining game," he said, "and right after the game I thought it had been a terrific game. But after watching the film, I saw that both teams had played great offensively but both had spent all their energy on the offensive end. Neither team played well defensively. For that reason I would not say it was a great game."

During a tournament there is very little time to prepare for an opponent, but both Kentucky and Arkansas knew each other intimately. Pitino told his players that they must concentrate on stopping Corliss Williamson inside and Scotty Thurman from the perimeter. He also talked about what the Razorbacks like to do. "They like to run out on the break and they will give you a chance to get the offensive rebounds. We had to get those. We also had to knock down our shots. We were a very inconsistent shooting team so we needed to work the ball inside and if there was nothing there, we had to kick it back out and hit from the perimeter."

Tony Delk's drive and basket kicked off a second-half Kentucky rally,
which saw the Cats come back and send the game into overtime.

Both Kentucky and Arkansas had large contingents among better than 30,000 fans who packed into Atlanta's Georgia Dome for the rematch. Everyone was expecting another classic between these two adversaries and the Hogs and Cats lived up to the advance billing.

Pitino has always insisted that it doesn't matter which players start for the Wildcats, but the ones who are playing the best will be in the game at the end. He had more or less settled on a starting lineup of Rodrick Rhodes and Walter McCarty at the forwards, Andre Riddick at center and Tony Delk and Jeff Sheppard at the guards. But the biggest reason the Cats were performing so well at that time was the big contribution Rick was getting from his bench. Freshman Antoine Walker was having a superb tournament and had come off the bench to lead the Cats in scoring the previous night against Florida. Mark Pope had done the same against the Gators to lead UK in rebounding. Anthony Epps was giving Kentucky good leadership when he came in to play the point guard position. Jared Prickett played well and Chris Harrison had become the player to come in when the Cats hit a shooting slump and get them going again.

The crowd was roaring in great anticipation of the game as the two teams went at it. Kentucky took the early lead when Riddick was fouled trying to get off a shot and the senior center, not exactly the world's best free throw shooter, went to the line and made both to push the Cats ahead 2-0. The game was only nine seconds old.

That was the last time UK would celebrate until very late in the game. The Hogs took the game over and with nine minutes left in the first half they had pushed the lead out to 19 points, 35-16.

"Arkansas felt that they could beat us," Pitino remembered. "They came out with great confidence because the prior year we had beaten them in the SEC Tournament and they were going to make sure that didn't happen again. They really came out with great fire in their belly."

True, the Hogs were playing excellent basketball at that point, but Pitino insists that, even though his team was trailing by 19, the Cats weren't close to panic. "In our style of play we always come back. Arkansas is not a ball control team and they'll let us back in the game if we make some shots. The lead didn't bother me as much as I thought we were losing a little confidence at that time. I knew we would make a comeback. I just hoped it was enough."

With the Cats 19 down, Chris Harrison entered the lineup and immediately got into the offense by drilling an eight-foot jumper. Rhodes followed with a baseline jump shot and the Cats had whittled the lead to 15. Arkansas never again matched its 19-point lead, but the Hogs had a comfortable margin most of the first half.

With less than five minutes remaining, Arkansas held a 12-point advantage, leading 42-30. Walker made a marvelous move, taking Thurman on the drive along the baseline to go in for a dunk. Prickett added two free throws and the Cats had cut the lead to eight, 42-34, the closest they had been in an eternity.

Thurman pushed it back out to an 11-point lead, but once again it was Walker to the rescue as he drove in for a basket. Pope followed with a three and the score was 45-39, Arkansas still led.

The Hogs rallied again, scoring the next five points, and with just over a minute to play in the first half, Arkansas was up, 50-39.

There was no quit in the Cats this day. Prickett got under for a layup and with just two seconds to go, Epps hit a jump shot from eight feet out and was fouled. He made the free throw and the two teams went to the dressing room with Arkansas leading 50-44. Kentucky had cut that 19-point deficit down to six points at the half.

"We were back in the game where we wanted to be," Pitino said, "but we still had to concentrate on the same things for the second half. We had to stop Thurman from the outside and Corliss Williamson inside and we still had to get more easy baskets off our defense."

Kentucky made several moves toward the Hogs, cutting the lead to three at one point, but each time Arkansas was able to rally.

The inside action was fierce when Arkansas and Kentucky got together to decide who would take the 1995 SEC Tournament title.

After Williamson's basket with 7:14 to play, Arkansas led by nine, 74-65. Kentucky was about to make its big charge.

Tony Delk drove inside and the big Arkansas frontline switched off to pick him up. He continued past the basket and made a reverse layup. Corey Beck fouled Walker and the freshman, having the game of his brief career, calmly dropped in both shots. McCarty smashed home a rim-rattling dunk and the Arkansas lead was down to three, 74-71. There was still 4:11 left in the game.

After Thurman's basket pushed the Razorbacks back out by five, Walker again took his turn at the free throw line and made them both. Beck did the same for the Hogs, and Arkansas had a 78-73 edge with 3:13 left.

With 2:29 to play, it was time for Walker to come through again. He glided down the lane and missed a shot. Have no fear, Walker was right there to grab the rebound and stick it back in, Arkansas 78, Kentucky 75.

The Cats finally caught up at 78-78 when McCarty drove in for a layup and was fouled. The junior converted to gain a three-point play the old fashioned way. Arkansas relinquished the lead only briefly. Williamson drove for a basket to boost the Razorbacks back on top 80-78.

With 22 seconds to go, Mark Pope got his turn at the free throw stripe for two shots. He made them both and once again it was all even, 80-80.

Arkansas brought the ball downcourt for the last shot. To no one's surprise, the Hogs worked it inside to Williamson. The Kentucky defense swarmed all over him and Corliss took the only option open to him. He passed the ball back outside. Enter Walker. He picked off the pass and Kentucky had possession of the ball with 5.5 seconds to play. Score tied. A timeout was called. Pitino signaled for Rod Rhodes to go into the game.

"I went to Rod," Pitino said, "because he was the best interior passer we had. I wanted him to create a drive to the basket so that he could find somebody open or create a foul. He was a very good free throw shooter. I didn't actually call the play until I saw the Arkansas defense. We have a play that we call a 'box set' and you don't know who's getting the basketball until you read the defense. After looking at Arkansas' defensive set we knew that Rod could get the ball inbounds. We called out 'Ice' and Rod drove into the lane and drew the foul."

There were 1.3 seconds to go. The score was tied 80-80. Rhodes had two shots. If he made one, the victory belonged to Kentucky.

Anthony Epps had been watching from the bench as his teammates battled back. Each time a Wildcat went to the charity line, Epps would cross all his fingers on both hands. It is debatable how much influence that had on the outcome, but the Kentucky players had been perfect at the line down the stretch. As Rhodes put his toe to the stripe, Epps could not bear to look. He turned his backside to the court and buried his head in his hands. Presumably, he still had his fingers crossed.

Rhodes was handed the basketball by the official. He put up the first of two shots. It was close but fell off the left side. No good.

Rod, an excellent free throw shooter who was connecting on 77 percent of his free throws, surely would hit the second and hand the Wildcats the victory. This was to be the cruelest moment in Rhodes' checkered career at UK. The second shot was short, falling off the front of the rim. Overtime.

"I thought Rod would make one of the two," Pitino remembered, "but he didn't. But he got us in position to win the game and that's what we wanted him to do. The only bad thing about it was that it swung the momentum to Arkansas."

Pitino was trying to get his players together, but they were devastated. "At that point Rod was sobbing uncontrollably. We spent the whole time trying to get him out of it. I realized I couldn't put him back in the game. He just couldn't stop crying."

Rick had been right. Arkansas clearly had the momentum as the overtime session got underway. The Hogs scored the first seven points and 11 of the first 13 in the extra five-minute session.

With only 1:39 to play, the Razorbacks held a nine-point advantage, 91-82, and UK apparently was out of the game. "It wasn't like being down 31 to LSU with 15 minutes to go because here we not only had a big margin to overcome, but we didn't have any time left on the clock. At that point it looked bleak." It did indeed, but this Cat of nine lives had one more to use up.

Walker got loose on a fast break and made the layup. Williamson fouled him and departed with his fifth foul and 22 points. Walker converted at the free throw line to cut Kentucky's deficit to 91-85. There was 1:33 to go. Arkansas mishandled the inbounds pass under heavy UK pressure and Pope came up with a tip-in and the scoreboard read: Arkansas 91, Kentucky 87.

Clint McDaniel cashed in a pair of free throws to push the Razorbacks back out by six, 93-87.

Delk, who had drawn a blank in six shots from three-point range, came through when it counted. Tony connected from 21

The celebration was on after the Cats heart-stopping comeback, which saw them erase a nine-point Arkansas advantage with 1:39 left in the overtime period to take a 95-93 win.

feet for a three and cut the Arkansas lead to three, 93-90. Only 41 ticks were left on the clock.

With 25 seconds left, it was Walker's turn again. He posted up down low and moved under for a basket. It capped his career-high 23-point game that was to help earn him the tournament's Most Valuable Player award. Pitino called it the best performance by a freshman, in a big game, he had ever seen. Still, the Cats were down by one, 93-92.

It was up to Anthony Epps to turn in what Pitino thought was the biggest play of the game. Scotty Thurman took the inbounds pass for Arkansas and was hit immediately by a Kentucky trap. Thurman tried to get the pass away to Beck but Epps anticipated the play to perfection, knifed into the passing lane, and made the interception. Anthony raced in with a shot that was wide of the mark but he took his own rebound and was fouled as he attempted to put it back in. Epps was a perfect two-for-two from the line. Kentucky, which had not led since Andre Riddick's two free throws nine seconds into the game, was finally in front 94-93. The Georgia Dome clock showed there was still 19.3 seconds to play, an eternity in a game like this. Everybody in the big arena knew that Arkansas' Mr. Clutch, Scotty Thurman, would take the last shot.

"We were not going to get beat by Thurman again as we did at Arkansas," Pitino said. He decided that Walker would guard Thurman and he warned his freshman star that Thurman would drive into him then push back to get his shot. Walker was taller than Thurman and just as quick. It proved a masterful move. Thurman raced down court and well behind the three-point arc, he went up for his shot. Walker, with his gigantic wingspan, had a hand right in his face. The shot fell hopelessly off the rim. Kentucky grabbed the rebound and Delk was fouled. He made one of two free throws to complete the scoring. Kentucky had won one of the most dramatic victories in its history. The scoreboard blinked the tale. Kentucky 95, Arkansas 93.

There was a wild celebration in the Georgia Dome but nobody

celebrated more that the Wildcats themselves. Pitino rushed onto the floor and embraced Epps in a big bear hug. The players were giving each other high fives and hugs. Everybody was consoling

Walter McCarty helps clip down the nets to commemorate Kentucky's fourth straight SEC Tournament championship.

the heart-broken Rhodes and urging him to take part in cutting down the nets. Delk picked up the plastic barrel of ice water and dumped it over Pitino's head.

It was the fourth straight year that Rick had led the Wildcats to the SEC Tournament title. In all, the Cats had won the trophy 19 times. But none — repeat none — had equaled this one for thrills, for excitement, and for sheer determination by a gutsy bunch of players to bring the trophy home.

The championship ritual of dumping a cooler on the coach's head moved indoors, courtesy of Tony Delk.